The Windmill
Summer Breeze Café

Po__ __ake is an avid scribbler of contemporary romance
an_ __coms. When not writing she loves indulging in the
__ __ __ail or two – accompanied by a tower of cupcakes.
T__ __mill Café series follows the life and loves of Rosie
an_ __ in the glorious countryside of Norfolk. Why not
pop_ __r a visit?

🐦 @p__ppyblakebooks
📘 ww__facebook.com/poppy.blake.395

Also in this Series

The
Windmill
Summer
Breeze
Café

Poppy Blake

A division of HarperCollins*Publishers*
www.harpercollins.co.uk

Harper*Impulse* an imprint of
HarperCollins*Publishers*
The News Building
1 London Bridge Street
London SE1 9GF

www.harpercollins.co.uk

This paperback edition 2018

First published in Great Britain in ebook format by
HarperCollins*Publishers* 2018

A catalogue record for this book
is available from the British Library

ISBN: 978-0-00-832436-0

Set in Birka by Palimpsest Book Production Limited,
Falkirk, Stirlingshire

Printed and bound in Great Britain by CPI Group (UK) Ltd,
Croydon CR0 4YY

To Mum and Dad; I know you would be so proud to see my name on the cover of a novel

Chapter 1

'Hurry up, Rosie, they need you outside to cut the ribbon!'

'But I thought our resident pop star had that honour?'

'It seems Suki Richards is far too busy scattering her celebrity stardust,' giggled Mia. 'Did you see the way Freddie was hanging on her every word? Yesterday he had no idea who she was, and now he's acting like he's her number one fan! Come on, someone needs to declare the very first Windmill Café garden party open or there'll be a riot!'

'Okay, if you're sure *you* don't want to do it. You've put in just as much work as I have – those Stilton and grape scones are to die for, not to mention the raspberry and prosecco cupcakes! Why don't we do it together?'

'Agreed! Oh, and by the way, you'd better have your best smile ready. When Dan Forrester from the Willerby Gazette heard Suki and her friends were staying in our luxury lodges, *and* that she had agreed to be guest of honour at the garden party, he jumped in his little MG and drove up here like Lewis Hamilton's older brother.'

Rosie hobbled in Mia's wake across the sweeping lawn at the front of the Windmill Café. She wished she had stuck to her usual preference of putting practicality over sartorial elegance and worn her ballet flats instead of the ivory stilettos with four-inch heels that sunk into the ground with every step she took and made her look like a waddling duck.

'I'm loving the belted tea dress, Rosie. That apricot-and-cream floral pattern really complements your hair.'

'Nothing complements my hair! It's the hirsute equivalent of jazz hands.'

'Don't say that. I know lots of people who would love to have your flowing Titian curls. Right. Ready to perform today's starring role?' Mia handed Rosie a pair of scissors and pointed to where Dan was lurking like a pugnacious paparazzo. 'Smile for the camera!'

Rosie forced a smile onto her lips whilst simultaneously cursing the Windmill Café's owner, Graham Clarke, for skipping off to his villa in Barbados as soon as the date for the first annual Willerby garden party was announced. His abandonment meant that not only had she been left with organizing everything for the party, but she'd also had to step into Graham's muddy Wellies to manage the holiday site in the adjacent field, and she had been battling her rising stress levels all day.

When Dan had eventually declared himself satisfied with his snapshots, Rosie picked up the microphone and tentatively tapped the end with her fingertips, producing a screech of bounce-back which caused every single guest to pause in their conversation and swivel round to stare at her and Mia. She ignored the pirouette of nerves that had appeared in her chest and cleared her throat.

'Hello everyone, and a warm Willerby welcome to the Windmill Café. It's lovely to see so many familiar faces. I hope you all enjoy the afternoon tea we have laid on for you, and that you indulge in a few glasses of the Windmill's own speciality punch made by my wonderful friend and baker extraordinaire, Mia Williams. So, without further ado, it gives us both great pleasure to declare the very first Windmill Café garden party open!'

Rosie grabbed Mia's hand and together they snipped the pale green ribbon to a smattering of appreciative applause, followed by an almost indecent stampede across the lawn towards the linen-bedecked tables that held the pretty three-tiered tea plates and china cups and saucers. The whole place looked exactly like any other garden party taking place in lots of villages up and down the country on a warm afternoon at the end of August. Triangles of pastel-coloured bunting and paper butterflies fluttered in the hedges, whilst wooden planters and terracotta pots, crammed with geraniums, had been dotted around the gardens. Tiny hand-crafted windmills in their signature peppermint-and-white colours rotated serenely in the breeze to add to the picturesque scene.

'I hope there are enough sandwiches to go round. Do you think I should make a few more of the salmon and cucumber?'

'Stop fretting, Rosie. Everything's perfect!'

Rosie didn't share her friend's optimism. Life just wasn't like that – or rather, hers wasn't. She often felt like she was one of those characters from a comic book who walked around with a rain cloud dangling over her head whilst everyone else basked in glorious sunshine.

Nevertheless, it looked like her luck might be changing at last, or maybe old Mrs Faversham, one of the Windmill Café's regular customers, *was* onto something. That day's sunrise had brought a clear blue sky and the barest whisper of a breeze. Perfect for an end-of-summer garden party, but not so ideal if you worked in a kitchen. And a tiny one at that. Well, what did she expect when she chose to earn her living in a café in a windmill? Bijoux was overstating it!

However, apart from the heat, she adored the quirky teashop with its circular whitewashed walls – inside and out – and the most fabulous sails that she had persuaded Graham to paint a cool peppermint green. Only, the colour choice wasn't doing its job today. Temperatures had soared during the last week and it was on course to be the hottest August on record.

Since moving to Willerby, Rosie had become an expert on the weather. She had to be. It was a skill required of anyone in charge of a café in the Norfolk countryside that was frequented by tourists, ramblers, and most of the patrons of the outward-bound activity centre on the outskirts of the village. What the meteorological gods had planned for any given day was a favourite topic of conversation and one she usually enjoyed discussing – except when the mercury recorded thirty-two degrees and she was melting like a discarded ice cream. She knew her cheeks were glowing – not an attractive sight alongside her amber curls.

'Do you think it would be rude to ask Suki Richards for her autograph?' asked Mia biting into a cucumber sandwich, her pinkie fingers sticking out at right-angles.

With her long mahogany waves held back in an Alice band

of daisies and dressed in a flared summer cotton jumpsuit, Mia looked every inch a Sixties flower child – despite the fact that she hadn't even been born then. As slender as a shop mannequin, she bounded through life with a smile on her face and a song in her heart. Her talents were many; not only was she famous for the lightness of her cheese scones, she also designed her own wide selection of aprons. She showcased a different one every day, mostly made from fabric she bought from market stalls. Only that morning, as they prepared to whip up a batch of the mini-Victoria sponge cakes for the garden party, Rosie had been forced to perform a double-take when Mia tied her apron strings around her midriff – only heaving a sigh of relief when she worked out that the pattern was, in fact, links of sausages and not something altogether more risqué.

'Maybe you should wait until later when everyone's finished eating, when the wine is flowing, and the vibe is more relaxed?'

'Good idea. Oh, hello there, vicar. Are you having fun?'

'I am indeed, Mia, thank you,' smiled the vicar, smoothing his palm over his comb-over before turning his attention to Rosie. 'The flower arrangements are absolutely wonderful, my dear. I particularly like what you've done with the bamboo. Very creative, I must say. In fact, the whole afternoon is an absolute triumph!'

'Thank you, Reverend. I am hoping that if the inaugural summer party is a success, Graham might be more inclined to change his mind about the Hallowe'en and Christmas parties I've got planned.'

'Gosh, you are a busy bee!'

'I just want to give something back to the village. I've only been here for a few months and already it feels like home. I want people to know how much I love Willerby and how grateful I am for their unwavering support. But tell me one thing. Is it always so hot here? I know I asked for sunshine this afternoon, but this heat is bordering on tropical!'

'Best be careful! If the weather gods hear you criticizing them, they may decide to take their revenge. We don't want a wash-out like we had at the church fête last month, do we?'

'Definitely not! I had visions of the holiday lodges floating out of the field like miniature houseboats on a tidal wave!'

As Reverend Coulson strolled away in search of a cup of his favourite camomile tea, Rosie glanced over Mia's shoulder at the upmarket holiday site behind the windmill where six luxury lodges – along with a gorgeous shepherd's hut painted peppermint-and-white – could be hired by affluent holiday-makers who craved a taste of the English countryside but refused to ditch the luxury lifestyle. Each lodge had been crafted from the best Scandinavian pine to produce a hi-spec home-away-from-home, equipped with SMEG appliances, Gaggia coffee machines, thousand-thread-count sheets and fluffy white Christy towels that were changed every day irrespective of whether the occupants had used them.

She sighed. How wonderful it would be to live in one of those wooden cabins, to be able to relax in the outdoor spa after a long, hard day slaving away in the café, gazing up at the stars with a glass of prosecco in one hand and a cookery book in the other.

But she couldn't complain; she loved the tiny, perfectly

circular studio that came with the job of café manager, baker, waitress, and reluctant washer-upper because Graham steadfastly refused to install a dishwasher. From her kitchen sink, she had an uninterrupted view of a patchwork of fields and woodland, stitched together with emerald hedgerows, and if she spun around one-hundred-and-eighty degrees, she could feast her eyes on an endless stretch of silver-blue sea sparkling with a sheen of iridescent pearls.

When she had walked out of her life in London, she had never in her wildest dreams thought she would be fortunate enough to live in a converted windmill. The flat was the ideal retreat for a heartbroken ex-florist who had left behind all the hurt and recriminations and, against the odds, managed to get her life back on track in a tiny village in the Norfolk countryside. She still sent up regular missives of effusive thanks to her guardian angel for returning to duty in the nick of time.

'So, Mia,' giggled Rosie, 'which of old Mrs Faversham's suggestions for a sun-filled afternoon did you try out in the end? Did you dance naked under a silver moon with marigolds in your hair? Or maybe you decided to go with rustling up one of her herbal recipes as a peace offering to the "rain nymphs"? Both are ridiculous, if you ask me.'

'Well, whatever your opinion of the dark arts, her magic seems to have worked! Come on, let's grab Matt and Freddie before they disappear. Maybe we can persuade them to help us with the tidying up and then we can all go for a celebratory drink in the Drunken Duck afterwards. I've noticed how well you and Matt have been getting on recently,' Mia added, an impish glint in her eye. 'Just say if the two of you would rather *be alone*.'

Rosie rolled her eyes at her friend and shook her head. Whilst she was grateful for Mia's easy acceptance of a new arrival in her friendship group, if she thought she was setting her up with the local Action Man, she would be sorely disappointed.

She'd had it with love.

Chapter 2

'Hey, Rosie, great party!' declared Freddie, hoovering up the leftover desserts like he was on a gastronomic safari. 'Did I ever tell you that you make the most amazing cakes?'

'Oh, but Rosie is a woman of many talents, Freddie,' said Mia, casting a surreptitious glance in Matt's direction to make sure he was listening whilst she listed her friend's numerous attributes. 'Not only is she a brilliant baker, she's a fabulous café manager, a demon organizer, and don't forget she used to be a super-talented florist in London. She was even commissioned to design the bouquets and bridesmaids' posies for the weddings of several TV stars.'

'Well, I wouldn't go so far as to...'

Rosie paused, uncertain about what to say. She didn't want to embarrass Mia by correcting her in front of an audience – and anyway, maybe Mia counted a radio weathergirl and a Sky Sports cameraman in her definition of 'stars'. But she was saved from having to decide by the arrival of the real-life celebrity in their midst who was clutching a bottle of champagne as if her life depended on it.

'Hi, everyone! Rosie, this is *the* best garden party I've been to in years. It's really kind of you to invite us all. I'm sorry I got side-tracked and wasn't around to cut the ribbon. I really must start honing my rapid extraction skills as well as my networking skills!'

'Thanks, Suki, that's very kind of you. I had a lot of help though, from Mia, from the vicar's wife Carole, and the ladies from the Willerby WI *did* help with the sandwiches. Can I introduce you to Matt and Freddie? They run Ultimate Adventures, the outward-bound centre in the village.'

'Hi there!'

Suki tossed her long blonde hair over her shoulder and held out her slender fingers to an awestruck Freddie, before turning her attention to Matt, her gold-flecked manicure glistening in the sunshine, her pink lips parted to reveal a perfect Californian smile.

'I hope you and your friends are enjoying yourselves in Willerby,' said Matt.

'Oh, we are! It's a fantastic start to a week away from my frazzled work schedule. When my boyfriend Felix suggested a luxury countryside break before the onslaught of all the hard work of a record contract, well, let me tell you, I leapt at the chance. The lodges are absolutely gorgeous, but next time I'm going to insist on staying in that little shepherd's hut. It's so cute! Anyway, excuse me, got to circulate!'

Rosie watched Suki make her way to the terrace in front of the café where her friends lounged on the peppermint-and-white painted benches, drinking champagne straight from the bottle, laughing raucously, and generally enjoying the sunshine and relaxation.

'So, Rosie, I notice we still haven't seen you over at Ultimate Adventures yet. What's the matter? Allergic to mud?' Matt laughed, cute dimples appearing in his cheeks.

With muscular shoulders and toned biceps from his daily involvement in the activities on offer at his outward-bound centre, Matt possessed that healthy outdoors kind of charm that attracted admirers and Rosie understood why Mia considered him to be perfect dating material. His spiky blond hair, the colour of honey, had been teased into surfer-dude tufts with a smidgeon of gel, but, when she took the time to look more closely, she could see a shadow of sadness lurking behind his dark blue eyes and she wondered briefly what had caused it. She had meant to ask Mia about Matt's relationship history but hadn't had the courage for fear her friend would interpret her questions as romantic interest. However, there was no way she was going to let him believe the reason she hadn't visited Ultimate Adventures was because she was some kind of pristine princess, even if it was true.

'Actually, I'm quite capable of getting down and dirty with the best of them.'

Rosie cringed when she realized what she had said and heat whooshed into her cheeks at the amusement she saw flicker across Matt's expression.

'So, you're a florist, are you?' said Freddie, oblivious to Rosie's discomfort. 'Did you design all these fabulous table decorations for the garden party?'

'I did.'

'And all the planters,' added Mia, proudly. 'Rosie's a floral maestro!'

A curl of pleasure meandered through her veins at receiving a second accolade in ten minutes. She had loved flowers and plants since she was a child, learning their Latin names from her father. Their demands for regular attention had become her therapy at the most difficult time of her life, then it had turned into her passion, and eventually it had become her livelihood. She had adored the little flower shop she used to run in Pimlico with her ex, Harry Fellows, especially creating the intricate bridal bouquets and brides-maids' posies.

Sadly, her long-held ambition to become a celebrity wedding florist had morphed into a nightmare, and Love Lies Bleeding had become her flower of choice until she arrived in Willerby with only a suitcase to her name. The little Windmill Café had gently unwrapped the mantle of misery from her shoulders, and the warmth of the friends she'd made here had helped to plaster over the cracks in her heart so that now she greeted every day with a smile on her face. She was so grateful to have her life back on track at last and she would never do anything that would jeopardize that.

'Ah, now I understand your "getting down and dirty" comment!' grinned Matt, a flicker of mischief appearing in his eyes. 'If you're interested, perhaps you can let Freddie take you on a guided walk through the grounds of Ultimate Adventures. There's lots of flora and fauna, but I don't think you'll find anything suitable for your table decorations, though.'

'Sounds like a great idea,' said Rosie, thinking it was a much better proposition than going all Tarzanesque on a zip wire through the treetop canopy. 'I might take you up on that, Freddie.'

'No problem. You might be the go-to girl for upmarket bridal flowers, but I'm your man when it comes to *wild* flowers. Wild flowers can be just as beautiful as any other, but you need to be careful what you touch. Some are toxic, not just to animals, but to humans, too. Laburnum, foxgloves, oleander, belladonna, ingesting just a small amount could kill you.'

'Is that true?' Mia's eyes widened and she ran her palms up and down her forearms to eradicate the goose bumps that had appeared.

'Deadly!'

Unlike Matt who had stuck to his work attire of figure-hugging black jeans and matching Ultimate Adventures logo-ed T-shirt, Freddie looked positively jaunty sporting a pair of smart navy trousers and a lime green polo shirt which accentuated the colour of his eyes – a prophetic choice as it did not clash with his hair, the colour of a fox's tail. He looked like he had just stepped from the deck of his luxury yacht.

'Gosh, I had no idea you could *die* from touching flowers! Rosie, what if I've inadvertently put one of those wild flowers in our table arrangements? Oh my God, our garden party guests are going to die in agony and it'll be all my fault!'

Rosie laughed. 'Don't worry, I think we're safe, Mia.'

'God, where's the prosecco? I need a top-up!'

Mia rushed off to the makeshift wine bar, with a chuckling Freddie lolloping in her wake, and Rosie and Matt sauntered after them. Suki was there too, ordering another bottle of chilled champagne.

'Rosie, my sister Jess has suggested I perform a few songs later. Do you mind?'

'Wow, awesome!' declared Freddie, nodding emphatically in Rosie's direction.

'That would be wonderful, Suki, but do you really want to sing? I thought you were here to relax?'

'I am, but it's been such a beautiful afternoon, I thought I'd practise a couple of the songs I'm a bit rusty on before I go into the recording studio next week. Do you mind if I use the terrace outside the café?'

'Of course not. Do you need me to do anything?'

'Actually, yes. I don't suppose you have any honey in the café kitchen, do you?'

'Honey? Yes, I think so. Why?'

'I use it to make my throat spray with a few drops of peppermint oil. I can't sing without it and I seem to have run out.'

'No problem at all.'

Rosie led Suki to the Windmill Café and through the French doors into the kitchen. She was proud that she had directed the whole operation of hosting and catering for a part of over forty ravenous villagers with flawless efficiency. She cast a quick glance around the room and, as she had expected, the place was pristine. She heaved a sigh of relief. The marble countertops had been cleared of all culinary debris, polished until they sparkled, and the sharp bite of ammonia stung her nostrils. Mia had accused her of practically bathing in the stuff but ever since she had been forced to leave her beloved little flower shop in London, she knew she had reverted to the strange kind of comfort and calm she had always found in scrupulous, obsessive hygiene standards.

'Ergh, what's with the intense chlorine smell?'

Suki's exclamation took Rosie by surprise and a surge of warmth travelled from her chest up into her neck and glowed at her cheeks. However, the last thing she wanted to do was talk to Suki about her painful past and the cause of her resumed struggle with cleanliness, how making sure that everything was so clean it squeaked was the only thing that gave her the peace of mind she craved. To cover her embarrassment, she strode quickly to the cupboard above the fridge and removed a jar of Jarrah honey.

'Is this what you're looking for?'

'Perfect! Thank you, Rosie, you're an absolute life-saver. My throat is so sore from all the talking I've done this afternoon. I take a lot of stick from Felix and Nadia, but I can't even think about singing without a bottle of my spray in my pocket. It's sort of like my good luck charm. See you later. Eight o'clock on the terrace. Don't be late!'

Rosie watched Suki flick her hair over her shoulder and meander back towards her friends, clutching the jar of honey as if it contained the elixir of youth. For some unfathomable reason, a spasm of sympathy shot into Rosie's heart and she took a moment to contemplate the five people who had taken over the luxury lodges at the Windmill Café's holiday site.

Felix, Suki's boyfriend, was still conspicuous by his absence despite being expected for the ribbon-cutting ceremony, and whilst the others were certainly all fascinating characters, she had little in common with any of them. Suki and her friend Nadia clearly had more of an affinity with the contents of a drinks cabinet than an interest in either floristry or baking and she made a mental note to hide her emergency bottle of Gordon's just in case.

She liked Jess, Suki's younger sister, but despite being twenty-one, she acted like an immature teenager rather than an independent adult. She seemed to float along in a world of her own, happy to follow in her boyfriend Lucas's wake like an excitable puppy on its first walk on the beach.

Rosie had already had to fight to keep Lucas out of the café kitchen. The first thing he had told her when they'd checked in at the lodges was that one day he hoped to be the proud owner of a Michelin star. The guy seemed to have modelled his entire life, as well as his physical appearance, on becoming the next version of the Naked Chef, right down to his accent – strange, because Lucas had also told her he was from Cornwall, not Essex.

Finally, her eyes came to rest on William, Suki's tall, dark and handsome music manager, who also happened to be Nadia's boyfriend. He stood a little apart from the group, as if watching a bunch of toddlers enjoying an afternoon cavorting in the playground. Rosie was grateful that there was at least one sensible person in their group otherwise she suspected the whole party could quite easily descend into disarray – something she wasn't good at coping with.

Chapter 3

After saying her goodbyes to everyone who had attended the very first Windmill Café garden party, Rosie grabbed a roll of black bin bags, handed one each to Matt, Freddie and Mia and they began to stuff them with litter. With the extra help, the tidying up didn't take long and by six o'clock a casual onlooker would never have known there had been a party at the Windmill Café that afternoon. She made a pitcher of homemade lemonade and slumped down next to Mia at one of the tables on the terrace for a well-deserved rest, whilst Freddie went off in search of a bucket of ice in which to store his beers.

'So, are you pleased to be back from your trek around the world?' Rosie asked Mia, enjoying the sensation of the cold, sharp, citrusy nectar trickling down her throat.

'Having a gap year is an awesome experience. I've seen some amazing sights, but there is nothing quite like being at home. Mum and Dad are ecstatic that I made it back in one piece. Mum's got me helping with the flowers in the church, as well as baking all this stuff for the Rev's homeless charity, and Dad's roped me in with the gardening and tending the

Poppy Blake

greenhouse. I don't mind, though. I'm still writing my travel blog and, of course, I'm loving working with you here in the café over the summer. Did Matt tell you he's offered me a part-time job as a zip wire instructor when the season ends in October – can't wait to start the training with our very own answer to Bear Grylls. And Freddie's promised to take me windsurfing and wild camping.'

'You can definitely count me out of those *very* special experiences,' Rosie shuddered. 'What's so enjoyable about getting cold, wet and muddy?'

'Oh, Rosie, wild camping is lots of fun! Actually, Freddie and I were talking about trying it out in Willerby Woods next weekend. We'll be foraging for all our food and water and sleeping under the stars. Why don't you come along?'

'Gosh, I'll take a raincheck on that if you don't mind!' she laughed as Matt and Freddie joined them.

'Rosie, do you mind if I make myself a coffee? Freddie couldn't find any ice and I don't think I could stomach another bottle of warm beer. Want one?'

Before Rosie could offer to do it herself, Matt had marched into the café kitchen and flicked the switch on the kettle. He spooned freshly-ground coffee into a cafetière with the careless abandon of a three-year-old in a sand pit, sending a generous scattering of the granules across the marble benchtop. Where only moments before soothing orderliness had reigned supreme, there was now a plethora of culinary chaos. Rosie's desperation to create order that always lurked just beneath the surface reared its ugly head and her fingertips tingled with the effort it took not to rush over to the sink and grab a cloth to start wiping away the mess. She chanced a quick glance at Matt, and saw him raise his eyebrows in amused enquiry.

'You okay?'

'I'm fine, thanks,' she improvised. 'Just tired. I hadn't realized how exhausting it would be to manage the Windmill Café as well as the holiday site, but I'm enjoying every minute of it.'

'So, too busy to come over for a flight on the zip wire, eh?' Matt's eyes crinkled with mischief, nudging her flagging spirits northwards. Every time she met up with Matt at the Drunken Duck, he and Freddie had tried to encourage her to spend the day with them at the outward-bound centre and she admired their persistence with a lost cause.

'I'd rather stick my hand in a meat grinder,' she laughed, trying her hardest not to let her eyes drift back to the spilled coffee.

'Not a lover of heights, then?'

Matt was right, indoor pursuits had always been more her thing, like flower arranging and baking up a storm. But, now she was settling into her new life in the country, far away from the city life and urban sprawl she had left behind in London, there was no reason why she shouldn't introduce a few changes, and start enjoying a more rural lifestyle. Wasn't life all about trying new things? Should she give the zip wire a go? A shiver of trepidation shot down her spine just thinking about it. Maybe she could begin with something a little closer to the ground.

'What else do you have at Ultimate Adventures apart from the zip wire?'

'Lots of things. We've got the climbing wall, there's the quad bike safaris, you could try paintballing, field archery, hover-carting, wild camping, and there's my personal favourite – the woodland obstacle course – although that's best enjoyed after we've had some rain. Which one floats your boat then?'

Rosie gulped. Each one sounded worse than the last, and the thought of having to choose between them caused her head to spin. What on earth was hover-carting? There was only one way to find out and with all-action-hero Matt at her side whilst she gave them a go, she suspected she'd be able to conquer all of those things – except the zip wire.

She sat up straight and pushed her shoulders back, met Matt's gaze and said 'I think I might give the archery a go.'

'That's great, Rosie.' Matt grinned broadly, his whole face lighting up with pleasure at recruiting a potential convert. 'A fitting choice. Has anyone ever told you that you bear more than a striking resemblance to that Disney character in Brave? Same unruly hair, same scattering of freckles across the bridge of your nose, same determined tilt of the chin.'

Rosie knew exactly who Matt was referring to. She had often been told she resembled Merida, but only because of her hair, not for possessing a penchant for using a bow and arrow when things got tough – although she had often craved a soupçon of the character's courage to get her through the difficult times.

'Yes, quite a few actually.'

'Okay, then it's decided, field archery, it is. I'll sort it out for one night next week after we close so that we can have the course to ourselves. Don't look so terrified. I know you're going to love it!'

She smiled at Matt's evident delight that she had agreed to ditch her doubts and launch herself into something new. Whenever she was in his company she felt more alive, more willing to take chances, to step outside her narrow comfort zone and into the excitement of the unknown. She wondered how he did it. Harry had certainly never made her feel like that, quite the opposite in fact.

'I think "love it" might be going a bit far.'

'Why do you say that? How do you know until you've tried?' Matt's voice had softened as he scoured her eyes for a clue as to why she was so scared of trying something different.

Rosie felt her cheeks glow under his scrutiny. How could she explain to the super-confident Matt, that two long years with Harry constantly belittling everything she did had taken its toll and her self-esteem had crashed to an all-time low?

'Come on let's take our coffees outside onto the terrace and enjoy the last of the sunshine.'

Chapter 4

'Hi, mind if we join you on the terrace?' asked Suki, a couple of bottles of prosecco poking out from beneath each arm.

'Of course not.'

Rosie smiled as her holiday lodge guests made their way to the adjacent table. Suki and Jess were giggling and teasing Lucas about his lilac jumper, a replica of the one Jamie Oliver wore on the cover of his current cookery book. Nadia, her auburn bob slightly dishevelled, was encouraging William to open another bottle of prosecco rosé from the crate of twelve they had brought with them. There was still no sign of Suki's errant boyfriend and Rosie wondered what had happened to make him so late.

'Looks like they've been drinking all afternoon,' whispered Matt.

Mia rolled her eyes, but Freddie decided to take advantage of the situation.

'Hey, Suki, congratulations on scoring a recording contract. I'm really looking forward to hearing you sing tonight! It'll be a real treat,' said Freddie, tipping his head back to drink from his bottle of beer, trying to appear nonchalant – but his cheeks were flushed and he was clearly in awe of Suki and her glamorous friends.

'Thanks, I'm stoked, but it's no overnight success story, you know. I've worked my guts out for this. Since graduating from music school in Sheffield, I've sang in some of the most decrepit and flea-ridden bars and social clubs in the country. That's where I met Nadia and William – oh, at uni, not the flea-ridden bars! Nadia's been my best friend ever since, haven't you, Nad?'

'Certainly have,' nodded Nadia, tucking her hair behind her ears. But Rosie detected a faint cloud of petulance pass over the woman's polished features, before she tossed back the contents of her glass and held it to out to Lucas for a refill. 'Ergh, it's far too warm.'

'Why don't I put a couple of bottles in the freezer for you?' asked Rosie.

'Great idea. Thanks, Rosie,' smiled Suki.

Rosie returned with two silver ice buckets, one for each table. But before she had the chance to plunge the remaining bottles of prosecco into the floating ice cubes, a blast of laughter exploded into the air. Lucas had stumbled backwards against the table, dislodging one of the buckets and drenching Nadia with freezing cold water containing bullets of ice.

'Stupid idiot, Lucas! Look what you've done! You've completely ruined my dress!' she screamed, holding the soaking fabric away from her chest in an effort to prevent the icy water seeping onto her skin.

'Sorry, Nadia. I'm not used to drinking this much champagne in the afternoon.'

'Prosecco, Lucas. It's prosecco, not champagne, you philistine!'

'Oh, come on, Nad,' soothed Suki. 'It was an accident. Look, why don't you go over to my lodge to get changed? You can borrow one of my stage outfits, if you like. I've brought a couple with me – help yourself.'

'Well, are you coming with me?' Nadia asked William, her hands on her hips, eyebrows raised, clearly mollified by Suki's generous offer.

'Not just yet, Nad. Why don't you get changed and come back outside? Show off the dress to us all?'

Nadia tossed another venomous glare in the direction of Lucas and stormed off towards Suki's lodge.

Rosie watched in silent fascination as the domestic drama unfolded in front of her. She felt as though, along with Mia and Matt, she was sitting in the stalls at an open-air theatre whilst the actors performed a short sketch solely for their benefit, especially when Suki flicked her blonde hair over her shoulder, removed her silver compact and reapplied a coat of frosty pink lipstick, beaming round at her adoring audience – mainly Freddie and Jess. She had to admit that Suki did look every inch the singing star. Perhaps her scarlet, off-the-shoulder dress was a little too theatrical for the terrace of a Norfolk café, but it was the perfect outfit for a celebrity-in-the-making.

When Rosie checked the group into their lodges the previous day, Jess had boasted continuously about the recording contract Suki had just signed after years on the circuit in Ibiza's cosmopolitan bars. She had warmed to Jess straight away; a free-spirit, a sprite of a girl, with no real comprehension of her sister's success, and she clearly inhabited an alternate stratosphere. She had even wondered whether the girl was on some sort of medication – she was sweet and fun, but vacant and scatter-brained. Rosie quickly chastised herself for her less-than-kind thought. There was nothing wrong with being forgetful – not everyone craved extreme orderliness in their lives like she did.

'Will Nadia be okay? She didn't look very happy about being drenched in water,' said Rosie, concerned that William hadn't followed her to their lodge as she had so clearly wanted him to.

'Oh, don't worry. She'll be fine,' said William, a flicker of irritation floating across his expression. 'But it doesn't help when Lucas starts teasing her.'

'Did you see the look on her face when the water hit her?' laughed Lucas. 'Ah, I wish I'd had my mobile ready. That would have been some ice bucket challenge for my Facebook page – seeing the uptight cow brought down a peg or two.'

'You promised you'd make an effort to be kind to Nadia while we're here, Lucas,' Suki reprimanded him. 'You know how she's feeling at the moment.'

'So what? If she can't be happy for her best friend's good fortune and insists on indulging in a childish spurt of jealousy, how is that my fault?'

'Stop it, Lucas,' interjected William, a sharp warning tone creeping into his voice.

Once again, that strangest of feelings swept over Rosie – as though she, Mia, Matt and Freddie were invisible, incidental onlookers. She saw Lucas flash his eyes at William, clearly considering some scathing retort, but at the last minute he made the decision to change the subject, although Rosie wasn't sure it was to safer ground.

'Anyway, where's Felix got to, Suki? I thought you said he would be here in time for the garden party. Must have been *some* reunion session with the lads in Colchester last night. Always did say Felix knows how to party. Not the old-ladies-style bash we've just been subjected to. Sorry, Rosie, but excuse me if I left my tiara and pearls behind in Ibiza!'

Rosie opened her mouth to respond but had no idea what to say so she closed it again, ending up looking like a gobsmacked goldfish. She caught Matt's eye and he smirked at her, rolling his eyes at their new friends' antics as Lucas snaked his arm round Jess's slim waist, drew her towards him and dropped a kiss on her lips.

'Had a little par-tay ourselves last night though, didn't we, honey?'

'We did!' giggled Jess, leaning backwards so she could coil her arms around his neck.

'But hey, Rosie, Mia, I must congratulate you both on earning your crowns as Queens of Culinary Excellence! I don't know who made those scones, but they were a-maz-ing! And you've got to give me the recipe for those raspberry cupcakes! De-lic-ious. I poked my head in the door of the café this morning and I saw you both slaving away. You don't know how lucky you are to have such great facilities – the windmill's kitchen is like a real professional chef's laboratory compared to the pokey crevice where I'm expected to perform my culinary magic for a discerning crowd of inebriated tourists.'

Lucas shoved the sleeves of his sweater up to his elbows and curled his upper lip in disgust at his misfortune.

'It's usually roast chicken and chips with a side of coleslaw thrown in, *and* there's always a constant litany of complaints. Hard work and talent count for nothing in the restaurants of San Antonio. Any monkey can heat up a beef curry in the microwave or fry a basket of scampi. That is *not* what I spent three years at catering college for.'

'Chill Lucas,' said Jess, trailing her fingers through his blond quiff whilst her own hair, woven with brightly-coloured beads, rippled in the late afternoon breeze. 'You're a fabulous chef. It's just a matter of time before your genius is discovered – then you'll get your own restaurant where you can do whatever you like, I just know it. I reckon you're absolutely on the verge of getting your big break like Suki has. In the meantime, you just need to keep working hard at that lobotomy qualification!'

A very unladylike snort erupted to Rosie's left as Mia spluttered into her glass of prosecco. She didn't dare look in her friend's direction in case she succumbed to a fit of giggling too, but instead looked on in surprise at the swift change in Lucas's demeanour towards his girlfriend.

'It's botany, you idiot. Not lobotomy.'

Lucas shoved Jess's arm away, scraped back his chair and stalked off towards their lodge.

'So, erm, Suki, where was your last gig?' asked Matt in an effort to lighten the mood.

'Nadia and I had a residency in a bar in San Antonio throughout the summer season and this year Will decided to come over from Majorca where his family live to join us, didn't you, Will?'

'I play bass guitar in a rock band, but I also get to act as their manager for my sins. I handle all the bookings and do all the paperwork. It was a contact of mine who had actually come to see *me* play who spotted Suki singing and put us in touch with a guy at Mountside Records. They loved her voice, and the rest, as they say, is history.'

'So, you were instrumental in delivering Suki's big break?' asked Rosie, understanding a little better why Nadia seemed so prickly. It would stretch anyone's friendship to see their boyfriend arrange their best friend's route to stardom whilst their own career floundered in obscurity. She watched Suki grab one of the bottles of fizz from the ice bucket and take a swig.

'That's right,' sighed Suki, wiping dribbles of liquid from her chin with the back of her hand. 'Will was the catalyst to my newfound fame and potential fortune, much to Nadia's annoyance. He persuaded the guy from Mountside to offer her a gig as a backing singer but she threw it back at him in disgust. It's one of the reasons we're here, actually – as an apology. I thought that if we spent some quality time together, doing something completely different, she would come round. To be honest, it was my boyfriend Felix's idea to come to Norfolk – although I'm not sure he's going to be my boyfriend for much longer. The selfish idiot promised me faithfully that he'd be here to help me cut the ribbon for the garden party. But, as you can see...' she swung the bottle in a wide arc spilling some of the contents on the terrace. 'No sign of him.'

Rosie completely understood Suki's irritation; Felix's absence had been the reason she and Mia had become honorary ribbon-cutters instead of their celebrity guest – not that she minded.

'Why *hasn't* Felix arrived yet, Suke? Has he called you to say he'll be late?' asked Jess.

'No, of course not. He's the most inconsiderate moron this side of the M25.'

Suki's eyes suddenly came to rest on Freddie as though she was seeing him for the first time. His jaw gaped open and Rosie had the distinct impression that a little drool escaped from his lips. She watched him clamp his mouth shut, slide his hands into his pockets, and scuff his loafers in the grass, raising his shoulders and elbows towards his ears in feigned disinterest.

'Hey, Freddie plays in a band, too, Suki,' said Mia with a mischievous glint in her eye. 'He's really good, too – had a very successful gig last month in our local pub. He adores all kinds of music, so I bet you have heaps in common. Perhaps you should get together to discuss the quirks of the industry sometime?'

'Oh, I think I can do better than that!'

As Rosie, Matt and Mia watched on in amusement, Suki drained the remaining contents of the bottle she was holding in one go. Steadying herself, she bent down to remove her stilettos, linked her arm through Freddie's and began to steer him towards the lodges in the field behind the Windmill Café.

'Freddie and I are going to compare musical notes and put a bit of the theory into practice,' Suki shouted over her shoulder.

'Hey, Suki,' Lucas called, a smile splitting his cheeks when he passed them on the footpath as he made his way back to the group. 'I hope you haven't forgotten you promised to sing for us before we go out for dinner tonight!'

'Of course not! I'll get ready and see you back here on the terrace in an hour!' Suki giggled as she stumbled through the gate, clinging onto Freddie's arm to remain upright just as Nadia appeared on the veranda of her lodge and performed a rather comedic double-take.

Freddie turned his head for a final look at his friends, his face a mixture of jubilation, trepidation and fear.

Chapter 5

'Do you think we should rescue him?' asked Mia, her forehead creased with anxiety as she swung her gaze from Rosie to Matt and back to Rosie again.

'I'm not sure...'

'Don't look so worried, Rosie. I'm sure your friend will be quite safe,' laughed Jess.

'What's Suki doing?' demanded Nadia when she arrived on the terrace, noticing William's eyes were still trained on the door of the lodge through which Suki and Freddie had disappeared a few minutes earlier. 'And was that Freddie she was with?'

'Yes, he's Suki's chosen suitor for an afternoon of summer delight. *Love is in the air...*' Jess began to sing before descending into a fit of giggles. She slipped her hand into Lucas's and stood on her tiptoes to kiss him on his nose.

Nadia rolled her eyes at their public display of affection before turning back to William 'What are you looking so glum about? It's me who got the soaking, not precious Suki. Felix should be here by now. If she gets caught it's her own fault.'

Rosie glanced at Mia whose expression morphed from apprehension to abject anguish. Again, she experienced the weirdest of feeling – of floating above the ground, looking down on their guests' interactions instead of being a part of them – and she was shocked when she saw Nadia pinch William on the arm to jolt him out of his reverie.

'I agree,' said Lucas, taking a long glug from a bottle of beer, all trace of his previous bad mood gone. 'Felix has had his fun, now it Suki's turn to have hers. Hey, Nadia, why don't you ask if you can do a number with Suki tonight?'

'Because we're supposed to be relaxing and having fun.'

'The two things aren't mutually exclusive, Nad,' said William, rearranging his facial features into something akin to sympathy. 'But I'm sure Suki won't mind if you want to perform a duet together. I see you helped yourself to one of her most expensive dresses. You know she was planning to wear that herself tonight.'

'She said I could choose anything I like, and I like this one. This emerald green enhances my colouring much better than Suki's, don't you think?' She twisted her hips in the sequinned sheath dress and patted her re-styled bob.

'You're gorgeous, Nad,' confirmed Jess, her ruby nose stud glinting in the sun as she swayed to the fragmented snatches of pop music spilling from the Windmill Café's open windows.

'Well, I reckon we should snatch a few more bottles of bubbly and grab a front row seat over on the terrace,' suggested Lucas. 'I know Suki's picking up the tab for the drinks today, but it'll be a drop in the ocean when she hits the big time, won't it, Will?'

'Shut up,' snapped William. 'Let's not forget that we wouldn't be here if it wasn't for Suki's generosity. Stop dreaming of being the next Jamie Oliver and get real. I'm off for a shower. See you in half an hour.'

'William? William...' Nadia called after him.

'Stay and have some of this fizz with us, Nad,' said Lucas, slumping down on the grass and dislodging the cork into the flower beds with a cry of 'whoop'.

'Mmm, it's delicious.' Jess laid her head on Lucas's shoulder. 'Don't worry, Luc. I think you're going to be even better than Jamie Oliver. Much more handsome, anyway. When Suki is famous, she'll eat in your restaurant, bring all her celebrity friends...'

'Oh, shut up Jess and pass the bottle,' snapped Nadia. 'Might as well make the most of the freebies whilst we're stuck in this dull backwater place. Sooner we're back in San Antonio the better. There're loads of luxury spa retreats in Ibiza, so why did Felix insist on us coming here? Oh, to think I could be soaking up the sunshine on your Uncle Ken's yacht, working on my tan with a selection of cocktails on tap!'

'Actually, you couldn't, Nad. Uncle Ken and Aunt Martha have taken *The Cortia* over to Sardinia for the week to meet up with Bart and Juliette for their daughter's wedding, or was it for their engagement? Or it could have been the birth of their first baby. Oh, I don't know. Anyway, they're not at their villa so that's why Suki agreed to Felix's suggestion to come over here.'

'Where is the sod, anyway?'

'You know Felix. Once he's in a session...'

'I think he's started to drink much more since he lost his role in that soap opera and didn't even get through the first round of auditions for the Renault ad. I bet his earnings from acting haven't even kept him in toothpaste this year. But if you ask me, it's a little like the pot calling the kettle! Did you see the way Suki was putting away the prosecco earlier? And dragging that guy she's just met off to her lodge? She's only doing it to get back at Felix and make him toe the line.'

'But Felix *won't* know, will he Nad? We're not spilling on Suki. She's the most fabulous sister in the world, and she's your best friend, too,' Jess reminded Nadia, her voice soft and dreamy as she cuddled into Lucas. 'Felix is just jealous of Suki's talent, always has been. Even more so now she's going to be a famous pop star whilst he's still waiting for his starring role in a Hollywood blockbuster. But he loves showing off at our villa, and down at the harbour on Uncle Ken's yacht, so he's not about to give that up, is he? *And* she lets him run around all the beach resorts in her Z4.'

'Did you hear what kind of car he's rented for the week here in Norfolk?' said Lucas, nibbling at Jess's neck. 'Only a Jaguar XJS convertible. Hope he lets me take it for a spin. Are you sure you can't persuade Big Sis to shell out for a car for you, Jess?'

'Eww. Get a room you two,' scoffed Nadia.

Rosie heard a crunch on the pathway behind her and turned around, expecting to see William. However, the footsteps did not belong to William, but to Felix. She had never been fond of verbal fireworks, and, seeing the look on Nadia's face, she decided it was time she, Matt and Mia left their guests to their own devices before the impromptu mini-concert started at eight. She got up and collected the empty pitcher and glasses to take back to the café, wash in hot soapy water and put away in their allocated space.

'Come on, Mia. We'd better get...'

'Hi, guys. Where's Suki?'

'Where've you been Felix? The garden party finished two hours ago – it's almost eight o'clock. You were supposed to be here at 2 p.m. sharp to cut the ribbon with Suki.'

'Can't blame me for giving it a miss, can you? The lads persuaded me to go to this new Sports bar – a little more exciting that this genteel granny's outing.'

Rosie sank back down in her seat. It was obvious there was no way she was going to persuade Mia and Matt to miss out on the live entertainment. She saw Felix flash his camera-ready smile at his three friends, displaying no ill-effects from an afternoon on the booze. His bleached-blonde hair looked as though he had just vacated the barber's chair – neatly cropped and sporting a touch of gel. His designer jeans hugged his buttocks like a second skin and his multi-striped shirt opened at the neck to reveal just a hint of golden chest hair.

'Hang on a minute.' Felix jogged back across the lawn to the car park and grabbed a box of craft ale from the boot of a scarlet Jaguar XJS.

'Is that Felix?' asked William, re-joining them and taking a seat next to Nadia.

'Yes, and it looks like he's brought another crate of beer with him so he can top up his alcohol levels to get through the evening,' said Lucas. 'Look at him. How did he even manage to steer that beautiful vehicle on these winding country roads without ending up in a ditch somewhere? Felix always was a lucky sod.'

'Someone needs to tell him that his drinking is out of control,' said William as Felix lurched back towards them, staggering under the weight of the bottles.

'Not just Felix with a problem though, is it?' said Nadia. 'It's Suki too. You saw her at the party – but that's the first time I've seen her hook up with a stranger. By the way, Jess says we have a gossip embargo. No spilling the juicy secret to Felix and standing back to watch the explosion.'

'Hey, William, my friend.' Felix grasped William's palm and patted him on the back. 'What's the word on the high-rolling manager's circuit?'

'You're drunk, Felix.'

'I think I'll make a cafetière of coffee,' declared Rosie, anxious to escape the soap opera. She signalled for Mia to follow her as she made her way into the windmill, but Mia shook her head, her eyes as wide as saucers. Even Matt stayed glued to his seat!

'Suki's promised to perform a couple of songs before we go out for dinner tonight.'

'Oh, goody!' said Felix, unable to keep the sarcasm from his voice. 'Can't wait for that unexpected treat. Yes, coffee with a wee dram should see me through one of Suki's gigs. I thought we were here to chill out, not to be subjected to another "I love Suki fest."'

Rosie carried a tray of mugs and two huge cafetières of industrial-strength coffee outside and poured one for everyone.

The sun was sinking towards the horizon, sending a kaleido-scope of salmon and indigo streamers across the sky on what had turned out to be one of the most exhilarating and exhausting days of her life – and it wasn't over yet.

The early evening air retained its warmth and the aroma of freshly mown grass and crushed lavender excavated painful childhood memories that Rosie had banished into the crevices of her mind and had not examined for a while, nor was she about to now. She checked her watch. It was 8.15 and there was still no sign of Suki getting ready to entertain them with a tune.

'Where do you think she is?' murmured Mia.

'Relax. Stars always take ages to polish their shine!' said Matt. 'And she did have rather a lot to drink this afternoon. She's probably sleeping it off.'

'Well, I'm not sitting here like a faithful lapdog!' declared Felix, tipping the final dregs of coffee into his mouth. 'If Suki insists on dragging out her microphone, the least she can do is be on time.'

'You've got to be kidding me! How can you say that when you've just arrived over six hours late?' said William. 'Look, I'll go and...'

'No, you won't!' said Nadia, pushing William back down into his seat. She obviously hadn't forgiven him for his lack of support in the ice bucket incident. 'I will.' She made her way to the edge of the terrace, but stopped next to the door of the café where Rosie, Matt and Mia were sitting. She glanced back over her shoulder at William, clearly hesitant about disturbing Suki on her own and regretting her refusal of his assistance. She recovered well, and smiled at Rosie and Mia. 'Would you mind coming with me?'

'Sure.'

Rosie and Mia got up from the bench and followed Nadia. Matt rolled his eyes and joined them as they made their way across the field to Suki's lodge. They paused on the veranda, Rosie and Mia exchanging anxious glances, fearful of what they could be interrupting after the afternoon shenanigans and the potential fallout it would produce.

'Don't you think we should knock?' asked Matt.

Nadia shot a quick look at Rosie and Mia, also uncomfortable about disturbing her friend's beauty nap.

'What are you all waiting for?' demanded William, as he came up behind them and elbowed Nadia to one side. He strode to the door of the lodge and knocked. 'Suki? Come on. Have you forgotten that you promised to sing for us on the terrace before we go out for dinner tonight? Everyone's waiting for you – including Felix! Suki?'

Silence.

Rosie met Mia's eyes. If Freddie was still in there, surely he would have opened the door to shoo them away. William knocked again, this time jiggling the handle and pounding on the door.

'Suki, wake *up*!'

Matt stepped forward, lines appearing in his forehead. 'Is there a duplicate key, Rosie?'

'Yes, of course, but...'

'Can you fetch it?'

Rosie's stomach lurched at the tone of Matt's voice and the genuine concern etched in his eyes. For what seemed an interminable few seconds, her feet felt like they were encased in concrete and she couldn't move.

'I'll go,' said Mia, sprinting off towards the café where they kept the spare keys.

William was now frantically banging his fist on the sturdy, panelled door. 'Suki!'

'What's going on?' asked Jess, joining them, with Felix not far behind her. 'William?'

'We can't wake Suki. Mia has gone for the spare key.'

Ripples of anxiety surged through Rosie's veins as a myriad of possibilities spun through her mind, each one more dreadful than the next. Within minutes, Mia was back, clasping a brass ring of dangling keys, pausing on the wooden steps of the lodge as she fumbled to select the correct one.

Felix snatched them from her. 'I'll take those. If anyone's going to intrude on Suki's privacy, then it's going to be me. And if she wants to have a snooze before we go out for dinner then surely that's her prerogative. Stop gawping!'

Matt moved to let Felix pass but William held his ground. 'We just want to make sure Suki is okay.'

Felix opened his mouth to deliver an angry retort, but the look on William's face prevented him from continuing. Instead, he slotted the heavy iron key into the lock and turned, a loud thud telling the gathering that the key on the inside of the door had dropped to the floor.

'Suki, darling, I'm back. Sorry about being so late, but you know how the guys get when... Oh my God!'

Rosie closed the space from the steps to the front door in record time and pressed into the room behind Felix, William and Matt. The sight that met her eyes would remain seared in her mind's eye for a long time. Suki lay on her king-sized bed, her legs curled into her chest, groaning in agony, her face as white as the windmill's walls.

'Call an ambulance!' screamed Felix, sprinting to the bed and cradling Suki's head in his lap.

'Suki!' cried Jess, rushing to her sister's side.

Suki's face held a waxy quality, her eyes glazed as though she had indulged in more than just an afternoon of alcohol. Perspiration bubbled at her temples and her groan had morphed into the heart-rending whimper of an injured animal. As Rosie watched on in horror, a spasm of pain gripped Suki and she crunched forward, vomiting on Felix's lap before relaxing back against Jess, some of her earlier colour returning to her face. A few moments later, her eyes seemed brighter and she managed a weak smile for her sister.

Rosie felt a movement at her elbow and turned to look at Mia. She was so pale she looked like she'd just rolled off a pathologist's slab. Her lips were moving but Rosie couldn't hear what she was saying so she tipped her head towards her.

'Mia?'

'Oh my God, Rosie! I think we might have just poisoned our first celebrity guest!'

Before Rosie could think of a suitable reply, Mia's legs gave way and she crumpled into Rosie's waiting arms. With Matt's help, she settled her friend on the sofa, loosening the buttons at the neck of her jumpsuit and wafting her face with a magazine. A few seconds later, Mia started to come round, her kind, chestnut eyes wide with anxiety.

'I'm so sor...'

'Shush. Just take it easy.'

Satisfied that Mia was going to be okay, Rosie turned her attention back to Suki. Felix was still cradling her head against his chest and Jess lay next to her, their fingers laced, sobbing uncontrollably. Nadia and William hovered nearby, their expressions reflecting their shock of discovering their friend in such agony. Suki herself, however, had recovered her usual pallor, but continued to wince as the occasional spasm of pain erupted in her abdomen.

Relieved that the worst seemed to be over, Rosie surveyed Suki's bedroom. Even in such traumatic circumstances she had to fight to staunch the sudden compulsion to start tidying up. Apart from the wardrobe that was crammed to bursting with an assortment of glittering cocktail dresses more suited to Las Vegas than the Norfolk coast, there was a jumble of toiletries and a huge purse of cosmetics tossed on the dressing table. Foundation, blusher, eyeliner and lipsticks were scattered over the glass top, as well as a hairbrush, heated tongs and a glass bottle containing a pale golden-brown liquid – probably her precious throat spray. Suki had clearly been in the middle of fixing her makeup and preparing for her approaching performance when she became ill.

'I said no, Felix. I don't want you to call an ambulance, and I don't need a doctor. Stop fussing. It's just an upset stomach.'

'Food poisoning more like,' growled Felix, shooting a venomous look in Rosie's direction.

'We don't know that,' said Matt, the voice of calm amid all the hysteria. 'Look, Suki, we should leave you to rest. Perhaps you could have a think about what you've eaten today and give Rosie a call? I'll go over to the village to check if any of the other garden party guests have reported similar symptoms.'

'Well, if you ask me, it's obvious what's happened. I want the Windmill Café closed down immediately. I'm calling in the environmental health guys. Suki can't afford to get sick! She starts recording next week. Some relaxing experience this has turned out to be!'

'Felix, will you let these people leave so they can check on the other guests?'

Felix reluctantly stepped away from the door allowing Rosie and Matt to lead a still-shaky Mia onto the veranda and down the steps towards Rosie's studio apartment above the café.

Chapter 6

As soon as they had settled Mia on one of the overstuffed sofas in the café, she fell asleep, curled into a tight ball like a newborn kitten. Matt called Carole, explained as succinctly as he could what had happened and asked her to activate the Willerby grapevine to see if anyone else had fallen victim to a potential food poisoning bug.

The final gasps of the evening sun streaked through the windmill's windows sending a kaleidoscope of pretty colour through Rosie's dreamcatcher. She felt as though it was a slap in the face after the way the day has ended. All the hard work she and Mia had put into making the first Windmill Café garden party a success had backfired spectacularly. Not only was there a distinct possibility that she had poisoned their first celebrity guest with her baking, there was also the chance that Felix would follow through with his threat and call in the food inspectors which could lead to the closure of the café, if not permanently, then certainly temporarily.

Rosie couldn't hold her emotions in check any longer and an avalanche of distress flowed through her veins. Could she have been responsible for giving the whole of the village food poisoning? If so, it would not only be the end of her career in the catering business, but there was a distinct possibility that the Windmill Café would never recover from the negative publicity. And even if the café wasn't closed, it was hardly an encouraging advertisement for a friendly village café where just eating a scone or indulging in a toasted teacake could mean you'd be taking your life in your hands.

What would she do if she was fired? Where would she go to next? Was she destined to be a nomad, lurching from one trauma to the next? Had she been a fool to think that she had at last found a place amongst friends where she could be happy? Why did life always have to drop grenades in her path? First her beloved dad, then the debacle with Harry, and now the Windmill Café. What was Graham going to say when he found out? If he had to close the holiday site down as well, he would be facing possible bankruptcy because of her.

Hot tears gathered along Rosie's lashes and she would have succumbed to a bout of weeping if she had been alone, or with just Mia to share her distress, but she didn't want to crumble in front of Matt who always seemed to exude an air of practicality in the face of adversity. She didn't want him to think she was some kind of helpless female. She turned her back and, for want of anything else to do, set the kettle to boil. She grabbed the huge brown teapot from its designated resting place in the cupboard and three mugs, hand-painted with a windmill design.

'You know, Rosie, this kitchen is so clean it could be pressed into service by the local heart surgeon. If you ask me, there's no way any of the food you made for the garden party could have been contaminated with even a microscopic germ. You saw how much Suki had to drink, it was probably something to do with that.'

'I hope so. I couldn't bear to think that my food has poisoned everyone at the garden party,' she said, handing Matt a mug of steaming tea.

'It's far too early to be making any assumptions, Rosie. Anyway, where's your self-belief?'

She tried to smile, grateful for Matt's support, but she knew it didn't meet her eyes. Uncontrolled emotions continued to churn through her body causing her to feel lightheaded. She was ashamed to admit that she craved the indulgence of a session with the bleach, an almost overwhelming urge to grab a cloth and start scrubbing the already immaculate benches to wash away the non-existent bacteria that could have been responsible for Suki's illness.

She took a seat on the sofa opposite a gently snoring Mia, surreptitiously pushing her hands underneath her bottom and starting the counting exercises that her sister Georgina had taught her when her compulsion to clean was at its peak after her breakup with Harry. She knew Matt was aware of her discomfort, but he said nothing for which she was grateful.

One of the reasons she felt so contented in Willerby was because of her attachment to Mia, Matt and Freddie. But was everything she had achieved in overcoming her heartache after leaving London about to be extinguished with a flick of fate, forcing her to move on to somewhere new? If that was the case, she realized with a spasm of guilt, she hadn't fulfilled her promise to join Matt and Freddie for a day of high-octane shenanigans at Ultimate Adventures, despite their constant cajoling and encouragement. She met Matt's vivid blue eyes and saw a gentleness that melted her reserve. She suddenly felt as though she could say anything to him and he wouldn't judge her, especially now that she seemed to have been pulled into another drama that was destined to ruin her life.

All her energy seeped from her veins as uninvited memories of her relationship with Harry began to crowd her thoughts. She saw Matt watching her closely as she chased her indecision down blind alleyways, and suddenly she wanted to open up to him about the reasons why her self-esteem had been at rock bottom when she'd arrived in Willerby.

'The reason my confidence is battered is because Harry, my ex, told me repeatedly that the only thing I was good at was keeping the little flower shop we ran together in Pimlico organized and spotless. Of course, in a way he was right. I don't have any formal training in floristry, my educational background is in catering. It took me months of persuasion before he allowed me to design a wedding bouquet for one of our clients and he was so dismissive of my initial attempts that I nearly gave up.'

'I take it you didn't?'

Rosie saw Matt's jaw tighten and was grateful he was on her side. She could have done with a friend like him around when the worst happened. However, simply meandering the memory maze caused the familiar emotions of worthlessness to rear their obnoxious heads, and the muscles in her stomach contracted painfully. Yet, her time at the Windmill Café with Mia's constant cheerleading ringing in her ears had enabled her to understand that the problems she had experienced had been instigated by Harry's dismissive behaviour towards her and she was able to look upon the termination of their relationship from a totally different perspective. As her sister Georgina had repeatedly told her, what Harry had done was reprehensible whichever way you looked at it, and this gave her the courage to continue with her story.

'One of the first flower shop clients I was "let loose" on was a magazine journalist who wanted to renew her wedding vows. I spent hours researching her favourite flowers, peonies, and I managed to find one called "Bride's Dream" – a gorgeous, frilly white flower that I paired with baby's-breath and wrapped in glossy dark green foliage. Even if I say so myself, her bouquet was stunning. Harry begrudgingly said it was acceptable.'

Rosie could picture the posy as though it were nestled on the table in front of her. She had loved the photographs that Annika had emailed to her the week after her 'second honeymoon' in the Maldives. She had even printed a couple off and framed them, much to Harry's disapproval.

'But the best thing was, Annika loved the flowers so much she wrote a special feature on fresh new ideas for bridal flowers and asked me to design three additional bouquets to showcase in her article. I was over the moon! That article increased our business four-fold and as a result we started to get commissions from minor celebrities.'

Rosie paused, unsure whether she could go on. Recalling that painful time was making it difficult to breathe normally and her heart hammered a concerto of distress against her ribcage. Of all the friends she had made in Willerby, only Mia knew about Harry's infidelity, minus the details about how she found out – it was just too embarrassing. She saw that Matt was listening to every word she said, his expression serious, and she suddenly wanted to get the whole terrible episode out in the open. Maybe if she gave her demons wings, they would fly!

'I never forget things – it's one of my, erm... well, my personality quirks. I was on my way to meet a harpist at one of the West End theatres to discuss ideas for her bridesmaids' bouquets when she called and asked me to take a few flower samples to show her. I doubled-back to the shop to collect the beautiful white calla lilies that we'd just had delivered that morning and... well, imagine my surprise when I stumbled upon Harry getting more than a little acquainted with one of our brides underneath the chrysanthemums. Talk about saying it with flowers! The two of them were practically screaming it!'

Rosie dashed away a solitary tear in irritation. That sharply focused image had been imprinted on the insides of her eyelids for far too long. What had happened was in the past and she *had* moved on.

'Rosie, I'm so sorry.' Matt reached out to squeeze her hand and an intense burst of his citrusy aftershave made the corners of her lips curl upwards despite her sadness.

'Thanks,' she muttered, grateful to see the genuine empathy in his eyes

'You probably won't believe this, but I know exactly how you feel.'

'Really?' She attempted a weak smile. 'Did *your* ex-girlfriend cause the cancellation of a two-hundred-thousand-pound wedding? Because that's what happened. Heidi was due to say "I do" to a Greek shipping lawyer the following week. She had called into our shop to finalize the guests' buttonholes and apparently couldn't resist sampling *everything* that was on offer. Surprisingly, they're still together, although Heidi refuses to work alongside Harry in the shop. It was four months ago and whilst I no longer have feelings for Harry, I'm still working on my forgiveness skills.'

She would never forget the first words Harry had said to her when she discovered the two of them together – 'Oh, Rosie, what a surprise. I wasn't expecting you back so soon!'. She had later realized that it was indicative of how far her self-confidence had dipped when she'd only just managed to bite her tongue to stop herself from apologizing for her unfortunate timing and inviting him to continue. Instead, she had simply swivelled on her heels and taken the first train down to Hampshire where she had sobbed the whole sorry saga to her sympathetic mother and her furious sister. She had not set eyes on Harry again, despite his pleading for her to return to the shop to 'fulfil her obligations'.

When Rosie reconnected to the present, she suddenly felt lighter, cleansed somehow, of the residue of gloom she had been carrying around with her since that fateful day when Harry had gawped at her unexpected appearance in mute disbelief. She sought Matt's eyes, wanting to thank him for listening, and was shocked to the core when she saw the ragged torment scrawled across his attractive features.

But before she could ask him about it, he had shoved back his chair and strode over to the sink. When he turned back to face her, the anguish had vanished and she wondered if she had imagined it. However, she knew she hadn't, that there were things hidden deep within Matt's soul that he clearly wasn't ready to divulge and she had to respect that.

'Look, Rosie, we're going to get to the bottom of this poisoning mystery. No one wants to see the Windmill Café close its doors. People come for miles for your chocolate fondant roulade, not to mention your cherry and almond drop scones and the café's an integral part of the community now, right up there with the Drunken Duck and St Andrew's Church – just don't tell Reverend Coulson I said that. And didn't Graham say how happy he was with the Facebook advertising campaign you organized for the lodges? It's solely down to your hard work and enterprise that you're fully booked until the end of October.'

'Thanks, Matt.'

'So, I've had an idea.'

'What sort of an idea?'

'Why don't we investigate what has happened ourselves? You probably didn't notice with all the drama going on, but when we found her, Suki's lips had a very faint bluish tinge. If that's right, it's definitely a sign of some sort of poisoning. We know there's no way Suki could have been poisoned by anything that came out of the Windmill's kitchen no matter what Felix says – so how could it have happened? Fancy a bit of amateur sleuthing to keep your mind off all those negative scenarios I can see churning through your head?'

'Really?' spluttered Rosie.

It was the last thing she had expected Matt to come up with. Yet her spirits had already notched up a level at the thought of doing something positive, and she could hear her dad's voice ringing joyfully in her ears telling her to go for it.

Chapter 7

Mia groaned, stretched and pushed herself up to sitting position. Her glossy waves had turned into chaotic curls and she looked much younger than her twenty-three years. She swung her wide-eyed gaze from Rosie to Matt and back again to Rosie as the realization hit her that the events of the last few hours hadn't been a dream.

'Is there any news yet on anyone else getting sick?'

'Not yet. I'll give Reverend Coulson another call,' said Matt and strode outside onto the café terrace.

Rosie had the strangest sensation that she'd been cast as an extra in a film; disconnected from reality, her movements those of an automaton as she forced herself to perform the tasks assigned to her by the director, of rinsing the teapot, tossing in fresh teabags and sloshing the milk into a jug. She located the sugar bowl and poured three mugs of strong tea, setting everything down on the coffee table in front of Mia.

Rosie tried to swallow down the hot tea, craving its reassuring warmth, but her throat felt like it had contracted around a miniature pineapple. Thoughts ricocheted around her brain about Matt's suggestion that they investigate the cause of Suki's

illness themselves. Little did he know that one of her childhood obsessions had been detective novels and that she had
spent many a happy afternoon with her father racing through
the pages until the culprit was unveiled - usually whilst in a
drawing room of a Georgian manor house. But this wasn't
fiction, it was real life!

'I can't just sit here drinking tea. I need to know what's
going on. I'm going to find Matt.'

She left the café with Mia, now fully recovered from her
fainting spell, hot on her heels. They found Matt striding
backwards and forwards outside Suki and Felix's lodge
winding up his telephone conversation with Carole.

'Carole and the Rev have managed to contact a few more
people who were at the party this afternoon and so far none
of them have experienced any of the symptoms of food
poisoning. In fact, everyone, without exception, has praised
the smooth organization and the delicious food. Carole told
me to tell you that two people have even made enquiries
about outside catering for a wedding and an upcoming chris-
tening at the church next month.'

'Told you,' smiled Mia, squeezing Rosie's hand and rolling
her eyes at Matt's expression of disgust when he mentioned
the word 'wedding'. Rosie noticed Matt's strange reaction and
filed it away for future exploration when the current crisis
was over. She had no idea when that would be, or indeed
whether she would even get the chance.

'It's not all good news, though. Felix has insisted on Suki
being checked over because she's still experiencing stomach
cramps, so Dr Bairstow is on his way over.'

'Do you think...' Mia paused, flashing a quick look at the windows of the lodge where the blinds had been drawn. 'I'm probably way out of line here, but do you think Suki could have taken something to... erm... well... to give her confidence a bit of a boost for the show she was going to put on for us tonight, and maybe she just accidentally took a bit too much?'

'Actually, Suki doesn't do drugs,' came a small, tremulous voice from the veranda above their heads.

Mia's face flooded with heat. 'Oh, I didn't mean... I wasn't implying...'

'It's okay,' said Jess, moving out of her hiding place on the veranda and slumping down on the bottom step like a lost waif, her eyes bloodshot from shedding copious tears over her sister's suffering. 'Lots of people in the music industry use some form of performance enhancement, I know that, but not Suke. She's totally clean.'

'But maybe she just ...' persisted Mia, as Rosie took a seat next to Jess.

'No, she wouldn't. She just wouldn't. I know her. Suki doesn't do *any* drugs. Not even paracetamol.'

'Well, hopefully the doctor will be able to throw more light on what's caused her illness,' said Matt, pointing to Dr Bairstow's black Range Rover pulling into the Windmill Café's car park.

Rosie watched the popular village doctor jump out of the driver's seat and rush round to the passenger side to collect his bag of tricks. He had clearly been disturbed whilst indulging in his favourite past-time because he was still wearing his rugby strip, tracksuit bottoms, and trainers.

'Have you contacted your parents to let them know what's happened?' asked Matt.

'Our parents passed away in a helicopter crash when I was ten. We've only got each other – and our uncle and aunt. They're on their yacht in Sardinia at the moment. Oh God, Auntie Martha's going to be so worried,' Jess squeaked, crumpling into Rosie's arms, her delicate shoulders heaving, her long wavy hair falling over her face.

The doctor's arrival had forced everyone but Felix to vacate the lodge so Suki could be examined in private. Lucas, William and Nadia joined them outside on the veranda, their eyes fixed on an indeterminate point in the distance rather than looking at Rosie and Mia, who they clearly still thought had poisoned their friend.

Rosie swallowed down hard on her distress about her uncertain future to concentrate on the misery Suki was suffering, sending up a prayer for a speedy diagnosis and recovery. Matt caught her eye, gestured for her and Mia to follow him, and they made their way back to the café terrace. Rosie headed for one of the wooden benches, which in the daytime was usually crammed with ravenous customers, and sat down. Mia slid into a seat opposite her and Matt perched on the table, a faint whiff of his lemony cologne floating on the warm evening air.

'I know it's too early to speculate, but I really don't think this is food poisoning. We all ate at the garden party, and no one else in Suki's party or in the village has reported similar symptoms.'

'So you think Suki's suffering from some kind of sickness bug?' asked Mia.

'Mmm, maybe, but there could be another explanation too.'

'What do you mean?' asked Rosie, her stomach performing a swift flip-flop.

Matt's forehead creased into parallel lines as he worked through his new theory. 'Why don't you tell me what you know about Suki Richards? Who she is, why she's here, everything.'

'I don't know much more than you, really.'

Rosie felt flustered, her mind suddenly washed clean under the intensity of Matt's questions. Obviously, he had meant what he said when he'd suggested they investigate the suspected food-poisoning incident themselves. She selected a strand of hair, twisting it rhythmically between her fingers, as she scoured her sluggish brain for a place to start.

'She's here with her sister and a group of friends to celebrate the signing of her recording contract. She's been singing in bars in Majorca and Ibiza since she left music school and this is her big break. Oh my God, what if this affects her voice?'

'I think it would be unusual if there were any lasting side-effects from a bout of vomiting. What else do you know? Who booked the lodges?'

'That was Suki's boyfriend, Felix – apparently one of his friends came here last summer and loved it. Felix persuaded Suki to come as it would be her last chance to relax before the music business stole her life – his words not mine. He even asked us to order in a certain brand of champagne because it's Suki's favourite.'

'And did Felix pay for the lodges too?'

'No. Suki paid for everything. She wanted to treat her friends to celebrate landing her recording contract.'

'So, if it's not drugs or a reaction to overindulgence of alcohol, what else could it be?' asked Mia. 'Some sort of allergy to an ingredient in the food? Or... no...'

'What?'

'Maybe someone *put* something in her food? A deranged fan or a jealous love rival?'

'Mia, don't be so dramatic!'

'Look, there's Felix,' said Matt, jumping up from the bench and striding towards Suki's boyfriend who had left the lodge and was sauntering towards the car park, taking the opportunity to snatch a quick cigarette.

'What did the doctor say?'

'Exactly what I thought he would say. Some kind of poisoning. I'm calling in the environmental health inspectors and there's nothing you can do to stop me,' Felix said, reaching into his back pocket for his mobile phone.

'Well, that's entirely up to you, Mr Dawson,' said Dr Bairstow, as he opened the door of his Range Rover to deposit his medical bag on the back seat. 'But as you've just heard me tell Miss Richards, at this stage I'm unable to pinpoint exactly what she's been poisoned with. I'll get the blood samples over to the lab immediately, and in the meantime, you should make sure your girlfriend gets some rest and drinks plenty of fluids – and I don't mean alcohol – and that she avoids exertion until she feels stronger. She's been very lucky not to have had an allergic reaction to whatever it was she ingested. We could have been looking at a much more serious scenario.'

'What? You mean, like, she could have died?' Felix paused in his search of the internet for the phone number of the local council to stare at the doctor.

'I can't comment any further until I know more.'

'But it's definitely something Suki ate or drank?'

'Yes, either intentionally or accidentally. I'm sorry,' added the doctor sending a sympathetic glance in Rosie's direction.

'Are you saying that someone could have poisoned Sukie *on purpose?*'

'I'm not ruling out any possibility.'

'Have you heard whether anyone else in the village has experienced similar symptoms, Dr Bairstow?' asked Rosie, her voice wavering and not sounding like her own.

'No, there's been nothing as yet.'

Rosie spotted the large plastic bag the doctor was holding, containing the champagne bottle Suki had taken back to her lodge with her, two used glasses and a variety of other bottles. She experienced a mule's kick to her solar plexus when she saw the throat spray bottle was amongst them, followed by a wave of nausea as she realized the implications. What if the cause of Suki's illness had been the honey she had given her from the café kitchen?

'Hello? Is that the environmental health department? No? Well, put me through to them. Why not? Yes, my name is Felix Dawson and I want to report a severe case of food poisoning. Am I speaking to the right person? I don't want to have to repeat myself.'

'Thank you for coming, Doctor,' murmured Rosie, her emotions swirling through her body so fast that she felt lightheaded and disorientated. 'You *will* ring me if anyone else gets sick, won't you?'

'I promise to keep you informed. If it is food poisoning, then I think I'm going to be in for a very busy evening. Weren't most of the residents of Willerby guests at the garden party this afternoon?'

'Probably.'

'Well, whatever Miss Richards ingested to make her so ill, it was exceptionally fast-acting. The garden party guests would already be dropping like flies. I take it no one else in your party has experienced similar symptoms?'

'No.'

'Please try not to worry, Rosie. It's by no means a foregone conclusion that Suki's illness is connected to the food you and Mia, *and,* if I understand it correctly, the members of the local Women's Institute, prepared.'

'I really don't understand why you can't send someone down here immediately. We could have an epidemic on our hands! How will it look when it's reported in the local press that a concerned resident reported the matter and the council did nothing? Of course I know what time it is. How is that relevant? I demand that you... hello? hello? Imbecile!' Felix pressed the 'end call' button in a rage.

'Mr Dawson, rest assured I will be in touch should there be any further reports of food poisoning from the garden party guests. I will most certainly ascertain from them full details of what they ate and drank so we can narrow down the possible cause. Until then, I suggest you utilize your energy by ensuring Miss Richards is well-hydrated and continues to rest.'

Rosie saw a flash of irritation sweep across Felix's expression and she thought he was going to launch into an argument with the doctor, but at the last moment he thought better of it.

'Yes, of course, Doctor. All I want is for Suki to get well so we can leave this germ-ridden place as quickly as possible.' Felix stowed his phone in his pocket and marched off towards the luxury lodge he shared with Suki.

'You know,' muttered Mia, her eyes narrowed as she followed his retreating figure. 'I wouldn't put it past him to have poisoned Suki himself!'

'What do you mean?'

'Well, apart from his totally impersonal reaction to Suki's suffering – preferring to concentrate on calling in the authorities rather than consoling his girlfriend – what if he arrived earlier than we thought at the garden party and saw Suki disappearing with Freddie in tow?'

'Mia, you really do have an over-active imagination...'

'No, Matt, hang on a minute. Mia might have a point. Except, I don't think it would be *Suki* that Felix would poison – it would be Freddie. Oh my God!' Rosie's hand flew to her mouth. 'Freddie! Where is he? He was the last person with her before she was found clutching her stomach in agony! Has anyone told him what's going on?'

The three friends exchanged glances and shook their heads.

'We've got to find him. Come on! Hurry!'

Chapter 8

'We can't just go haring off. We have no idea where to start looking.'

'Well, I'm calling him right now!'

Mia scrambled around in her bag for her phone and selected Freddie's number. Rosie stared at her, fingers crossed in her pockets, praying for Freddie to answer with his usual chirpy greeting. But her personal deliverer of good news was off-duty, sadly not a rarity these days, and Mia's call went to voicemail.

'Freddie, it's Mia. Call me back as soon as you get this message. It's urgent!'

'We should at least go round to his house. What if he's lying in agony, just like Suki, unable to reach for the phone to call the doctor?'

The very thought caused a spasm of pain to slice through Rosie's abdomen. Just because Suki hadn't been allergic to whatever had caused her to become so ill, didn't mean Freddie, or anyone else for that matter, wouldn't be. Was the reason he wasn't answering his phone because... because it was too late?

'Come on. Let's try his flat first.'

They all jumped into the mud-caked SUV sporting the purple logo of Ultimate Adventures and Matt skidded away from the Windmill Café car park, sending a scattering of gravel and dust in their wake like confetti at a wedding. No one spoke during the five minutes it took to drive to the Willerby village post office above which Freddie rented a studio apartment. Rosie spent the whole time fighting her runaway thoughts that insisted on racing down myriad disturbing avenues of possibility.

When they arrived at the post office, Matt was the first to leap from his seat and together they ran to the front gate. The density of the summer foliage on either side of the pathway leading to his door drowned out all ambient noise, even the birds seemed to have taken a break from their nightly choir practice. Peace prevailed and the warm August breeze caressed Rosie's skin like a lover's whisper. For a few blissful seconds she felt as though there was no stomach-churning conundrum to unravel and they were just paying a friendly visit to Freddie to chat about his day at Ultimate Adventures. Sadly, her pleasant reverie was rudely interrupted when Matt began hammering on Freddie's front door.

'Freddie? Freddie?'

Rosie stepped back to look at the upstairs window, but there was no sign of life.

'Freddie?' called Mia through the letterbox, her face almost translucent in the amber light from the streetlamps that illuminated the garden.

Rosie hadn't known Freddie for long, but, just as with Matt, she had connected with him straight away. She would never forgive herself if anything had happened to him. But the uncertainty was tearing at her mind so much that if they didn't find him alive and well in the next few minutes she would be looking at her sanity in the rear-view mirror. All she felt like doing was opening her mouth and screaming, screaming until her voice cracked, but she knew she had to be brave and hang onto her emotions until they had the answer to the cause of Suki's poisoning – then she could indulge in a falling-to-pieces scenario.

Matt gave up pounding on the door and sprinted round to the back of the property, leaping over the white picket fence like an Olympic hurdler. Rosie and Mia followed him, managing to negotiate the fence in a much clumsier fashion.

'Do you think he's...' began Mia, hugging her arms to her chest.

Rosie slid her arm around her friend's shoulders as Matt searched beneath the flower pots for a key.

'Got it!'

Rosie followed Matt up the steep staircase to Freddie's flat, but a cursory glance told her straight away that Freddie wasn't home. It wasn't the typical bachelor pad – practical, functional, devoid of any real personality – but filled with gem-coloured cushions, throws and vibrant watercolours. She itched to adjust the furnishings, to straighten the picture above the mantel-piece that had been knocked off-centre, to wipe the dribbles of ash from the hearth, to clear the benches of the detritus of Freddie's breakfast, but she managed to rein in her errant impulses.

'What are we going to do?' whimpered Mia.

It was suddenly all too much for her and she burst into tears. Rosie dragged her into a hug, and with relief allowed the tears to fall down her own cheeks. Over Mia's shoulder she watched as Matt rubbed his palm across his jawline, his eyes sombre, his brain working overtime.

'I'm going to ring a couple of Freddie's friends from the band. Maybe he's with them, boasting about his dalliance with a famous rock musician.' And he ran down the stairs into the back garden to make the calls.

'Where do you think he is, Rosie?'

'I have no idea, but I'm sure he'll be okay wherever he is. Look, I'm going to ring Dr Bairstow to see if he's had any more callouts.'

Rosie tried to extricate her mobile from her handbag, but her fingers were shaking so much that she lost her grip and the phone tumbled to floor. She bent down to retrieve it and again, the feeling of light-headedness almost engulfed her, forcing her to slump onto Freddie's surprisingly chintzy sofa and wait for the moment to pass.

She needed to staunch the anxiety gnawing at her stomach for the time being, and ignore the fact that if she lost her job at the Windmill Café she would also lose her home. She thought she had moved on from the distressing events that had taken place in London, had even started to see an improvement in her compulsion to clean, but it seemed that dark grey raincloud had caught up with her again.

'Hello, Dr Bairstow, it's Rosie Barnes here. I just wondered whether there's any news on new cases of food poisoning?'

'None. I've called a couple of pals who were with you this

afternoon and they all told me that not only are they fit and well, but they thoroughly enjoyed the garden party and are hoping that you will organize something similar at Christmas. I've also spoken to my colleague in Hamsterly, Doctor Mullins, and he's having a very quiet evening, too – no callouts. I'm cautiously optimistic that the cause of Suki's illness did not originate in the Windmill Café's food. I promise to press the lab technicians for a swift result on the blood tests so I can completely put your mind at rest.'

'Thank you, Doctor, that's very kind of you. Could I ask you one final question? Have you heard anything from Freddie Armstrong at all? It's just, erm, well, he left the garden party with Suki and we saw them go back to her lodge. He wasn't there when Felix found Suki so we're worried about him. He could have eaten or drank whatever Suki did – we're having trouble contacting him and he's not at home.'

'I'm sorry. I haven't had any calls about Freddie. Suki didn't mention the fact she had a visitor in her lodge when I examined her. Of course, I understand her reticence. Have you asked Suki what happened to your friend?'

'No.'

'Then, I think that's your next conversation. If I can help any further, please let me know.'

'Thank you.' Rosie cut the call and turned to Mia who had been following the conversation. 'We need to speak to Suki. Come on.'

'But what about Felix?'

'We'll work something out.' Rosie ran down the stairs and joined Matt in the garden. 'Any news?'

'No one's seen him.'

'I've just spoken to Dr Bairstow. He hasn't heard from Freddie either, but thankfully there's been no more cases of food poisoning reported. He suggests we speak to Suki – after all, she *was* the last one to see him before he disappeared.'

'Okay. Let's go.'

Before they had even got back to the SUV Matt's mobile burst into life. Rosie watched on, her heart pounding against her ribcage, sending up a fervent request that the director of positive outcomes was back from her vacation.

'Okay, thanks for letting me know. We'll be right there.'

'Well?'

'Found him.'

'Thank God,' muttered Rosie and Mia in unison. 'Is he okay?'

'Well, he isn't writhing in agony from ingesting a dose of poison, if that's what you mean. However, he's really upset about what has happened to Suki and he swears he has nothing to do with it.'

'So, where is he?'

'He's at the vicarage with the Rev and Carole. He wanted to go straight back to the lodge to see Suki, to make sure she was okay, but bearing in mind Felix's temper, I thought it best if he stayed where he was.'

'Good call,' muttered Mia.

'Oh God!' exclaimed Rosie as something else occurred to her. 'I completely forgot. I should call Graham in Barbados to let him know what's going on.'

'I know it's not my decision, but why don't you wait until

the morning,' said Matt, climbing up into the driver's seat. 'Any explanation is going to be easier on his ears when you know for certain what caused Suki's sudden illness. The Windmill Café's reputation would take a hit if it turns out to be a food poisoning scare, but if she was targeted, then that puts everything in a totally different light – you can't be held responsible for that. However, I also think we should hold back on mentioning that theory when we talk to Carole. You can shoot me down all you want, but in Willerby, gossip spreads like burgundy wine on a cream carpet and we still can't rule out the fact that Suki took something herself. *"Singer Takes Accidental Overdose"*, well, no news there, is there?'

'Okay, you're probably right. I'll call Graham in the morning. Let's talk to Freddie and find out what on earth happened when he went back to the lodge with Suki.'

Rosie was still worried about the café, but doing something positive, like talking to the people involved and trying to piece together exactly what had happened, made her feel better, more in control of events, rather than simply succumbing to the feelings of disorientation and panic. As they made their way to the vicarage, a number of theories ricocheted around her brain: had Sukie taken an overdose? From what Jess had said, it didn't seem likely. And if it wasn't accidental food poisoning, all that was left was that Suki had been targeted by a person or persons unknown.

But who? And, more to the point, why?

Chapter 9

The handsome sandstone vicarage crouched beneath a canopy of trees, a battalion of arboreal obelisks embroidered with cobwebs and draped with necklaces of glossy ivy. With rectangles of amber light winking at its bay windows, the building took on the resemblance of a stone-hewn sailing ship moored against a backdrop of rippling leaves that undulated to the waltz of the wind. A solitary coil of silver smoke trailed from the chimney and merged with the night sky.

Rosie leapt from the passenger seat of Matt's SUV and sprinted up the stone steps to the impressive front door that Carole had chosen to paint a cheery red, closely followed by Mia. She raised her hand to press the doorbell but paused. Why wasn't Matt with them? She turned to look over her shoulder and, through the windscreen, saw him slumped over the steering wheel gazing at the entrance to the church on their right.

'What's wrong with Matt?'

'Oh my God! With all the worry about Freddie, I completely forgot!' exclaimed Mia, her eyes filled with contrition and sympathy. 'This must be the first time he's been back to St Andrew's since...'

Mia interrupted her explanation to rush back down the steps to talk to him through the driver's window. Rosie wanted to follow her, but the expression on Matt's face caused her to hesitate. He was obviously undergoing some kind of internal emotional struggle, shaking his head and making regretful gestures to Mia. Whatever had happened at the church, or maybe at the vicarage, to prevent him from rushing inside to talk to his friend must have been traumatic.

Rosie suddenly wanted to know the details, wanted to offer her support just as Matt had done for her when she had unburdened her own pain at the café whilst Mia slept. That dark haunted look she had seen earlier was now clearly etched in his eyes so she knew she hadn't imagined it. Had he lost someone close to him and the church held distressing memories? If so, she wondered who.

Mia continued with her persuasion, but Matt refused to budge, slamming the gearstick into reverse and zooming back down the driveway, leaving Mia staring after him in concern.

'Matt's asked us to meet him at the Drunken Duck.'

'But, why? I don't understand...'

However, Mia had pressed the doorbell and Reverend Coulson answered their summons immediately. He smiled in welcome and led them into the kitchen, the real heart of the home, where Freddie was huddled at the scrubbed pine table, his fingers laced through the handle of a mug containing something strong. He didn't look up when they joined him but continued to stare morosely into the bottom of his cup as if searching for answers in its depths.

'Freddie?'

'I didn't do anything, Mia! Nothing! Nothing at all. We just chatted about music for less than five minutes and then I left.'

'I know, I know,' Mia soothed.

Rosie loitered at the kitchen door, unsure whether Freddie would prefer to talk to Mia without her listening in. Just as with Matt, she and Freddie had hit it off immediately and she loved his quirky sense of humour and tendency towards comedic exuberance when he'd had a couple of beers. However, she also knew he was a softy at heart who would do anything for his friends and she knew that the shock of hearing about Suki would have upset him tremendously.

'Unless I can assist, I'll leave you in peace,' said Reverend Coulson. 'Carole and I will be in the drawing room if you need anything.'

'Thank you, Reverend, but Matt's waiting for us at the Drunken Duck,' sighed Mia, giving Roger Coulson a meaningful glance that conveyed everything to the vicar and Freddie and nothing to Rosie. 'Freddie? Are you up to joining us?'

Freddie raised his eyes to Mia's and nodded. He grabbed his denim jacket and followed them along the passageway to the front door, his whole body slumped like a puppet clipped of its strings. They bade goodnight to the sympathetic vicar and made their way down the gravel drive back to the entrance gate.

'What's going on, Mia? Why wouldn't Matt...'

'Later, Rosie.'

'Oh, okay.'

Rosie fell back a couple of paces behind Mia and Freddie, a little startled at the way her enquiry had been closed down. Mia's reaction reminded her that despite her deepening connection with Willerby, she was still a newcomer and after all, she *had* been probing for details about Matt's personal life which perhaps he would want to keep to himself. She understood that, but it made her feel like she was back in the school playground, excluded from the whispered gossip that she had always thought was about her after her self-confidence had dipped when she'd lost her father. But this definitely wasn't about her, so she ignored the nip of hurt Mia's words had inadvertently caused and strode forward to rejoin her.

The Drunken Duck was on the opposite side of the village green to the vicarage. Its whitewashed façade glowed with golden light from two large iron lanterns which also illuminated the large letters proclaiming its name. Mia pushed open the heavy oak door and guided them towards the back room. Immediately, Rosie was enveloped in a warm, welcoming hug of buzzing chatter, interspersed with the occasional burst of laughter, rippling against the background tune of a classic Beatles track. A faint aroma of yeasty beer, mingled with baked dough from the huge pizza the customers next to the fireplace were in the process of devouring, met her nostrils and she relaxed.

When they arrived in the snug, Rosie was surprised to see Matt looking almost as morose as Freddie. She ached to ask what was going on, but the priority was to talk to Freddie who had slumped down on the banquette next to his friend.

'Hey, Matt. Sorry about holing up at the vicarage...'

'Don't worry about it,' said Matt, visibly dragging his mood out of the doldrums to concentrate on the task in hand. He flicked a glance in Rosie's direction and she was gratified to see that the earlier sadness had been replaced by a hint of seriousness in his deep blue eyes.

'Listen, Freddie. Suki's boyfriend has arrived and he's got it into his head that Rosie's responsible for making Suki sick. Felix has called in the authorities and is demanding the café is shut down. If that happens, Rosie could lose her job and with it her home. Now, as anyone who's been in the Windmill Café's kitchen knows, there's no way Suki's illness could be down to careless food preparation and I thought we could help her by investigating the real cause. So that means you have to tell us exactly what happened between you and Suki when you went back to her lodge. No matter how intimate or embarrassing. If you would rather Mia and Rosie left...'

'No! Honestly, Matt, there's no need. Nothing happened. Is Suki okay? I swear to you, she was absolutely fine when I left her. Is it true what Carole told me? That someone may have tried to poison her?'

'It's a possibility, but Dr Bairstow says we should wait for the results of her blood test before we start speculating.'

'But how? Why?'

'All we know is that Suki must have become unwell at some point after you left. We don't *know* how or why. But,' Matt softened his voice and held his friend's eyes for a beat, 'it does seem you were the last person to have been in her company. You have to help us understand what happened after you left the party together.'

As Rosie waited for Freddie to explain, her heart hammered out a concerto of sympathy. Matt and Freddie should have been enjoying a well-deserved pint after a long week at the outward-bound centre and a stint volunteering at the Windmill Café garden party. She suspected they would be the first to put their names on the list when she was looking for help with her Autumn Leaves Hallowe'en party at the end of October – if indeed she was still around to organize it.

'Really, Matt, I promise you, there's nothing to tell. You saw what Suki was like. She must have downed at least two bottles of prosecco before we were even introduced. She was drunk, or so I thought. I was as surprised as everyone else when she dragged me off to the lodge like that. She's gorgeous, and it was great to meet someone who loves music just as much as I do. Believe me, I had no idea she had a boyfriend. I'm not sure what I expected to happen when we got back to her lodge. I'm not even sure anything would have happened. I'd only had a cup of tea and a couple of warm beers so I was in full command of my senses, and, call me old-fashioned, but I prefer my date to know what she's doing.'

'What do you mean "she was drunk, or so I thought"?' Matt pressed.

'When we arrived at her lodge, Suki disappeared into the bathroom. I stood at the window in the lounge. I just couldn't get my head around what was going on. I was struggling with my conscience as to what to do next when she emerged, fully-clothed and as sober as my Aunt Marjory.'

'What? But we all watched her swallow the entire contents of a bottle of prosecco,' Rosie said. 'How could she have been sober?'

'I don't know how, she just was. She offered to open a bottle of Moët she had brought with her, but I declined. Hate the stuff. I'm a beer and whiskey man, you know I am.' His eyes sought Matt's, silently pleading for his support. 'Anyway, panic had started to set in. I mean, she's on the verge of becoming a famous singer and who am I? No. I didn't want to get involved in anything like that. I swear I was about to make my excuses and leave, when she apologized.'

'For what?'

'For the scene she had created on the lawn. She told me she'd had to make it look like she'd scored with a handsome guy. Had to make someone jealous. Teach them a lesson, like. Well, I was so relieved I didn't have to explain my change of heart that it didn't even occur to me to be offended at being used as some kind of pawn in whatever game she was playing.'

'Then what happened.'

'She pecked me on the cheek and ushered me out sharpish. It was only as I walked down the steps of the lodge that the shame and embarrassment at being unceremoniously dumped set in. All I wanted was a decent slug of whiskey to obliterate the humiliation, so I doubled back and walked through the fields to the village. I called in at the flat for a bottle of Jack and went down to the office where I knew I wouldn't be disturbed. The next thing I knew, the Rev and Carole were hammering on the door like the world had come to an end.

They knew everyone was looking for me and they came to find me.'

'What time did you get to the flat?'

'No idea. Probably just before seven o'clock. I bumped into Carole when I was walking across the village green on my way to the centre. She asked if I was okay, I mumbled something about being fine but she didn't look convinced.'

'So, you must have left Suki at just after 6.30. It takes twenty minutes to walk to Willerby through the fields. When you were with Suki, did she complain about feeling unwell; nausea, stomach cramps, light-headedness?'

'No.'

'And did either of you eat or drink anything?'

'No. Look, I know what people might be thinking – that I put something in her drink, but I swear to you I didn't. I told you, she was fine when I left. She even locked the door behind me. I heard the click. Matt, what's going to happen? What if Suki wants to get the police involved?'

'Let's hope it doesn't come to that. We won't know whether or not it was an accident until the doctor gets the results of the blood tests back.'

When Freddie took a sip from his pint of Guinness, Rosie saw that his hands were trembling. His familiar healthy complexion was tinged with grey, dark smudges had appeared beneath his eyes and he continually rubbed his palm over his chin. Despite her own catalogue of anxiety, Rosie's heart ached for him.

'Look, it's late. I think we should all get some sleep and meet up again in the morning.'

Matt nodded his agreement, running his fingers through his hair so that it stuck up in random tufts, but his grave expression spoke of his concern as he asked 'Is it okay if I take the sofa at yours, Fred?'

Rosie saw the look of gratitude Freddie sent to his best friend and colleague and she smiled at Matt's kindness. Matt might look like a no-nonsense man-of-action-and-practicality on the outside – not to mention the added attraction of his toned physique and come-to-bed eyes – but on the inside, he was obviously a loyal and supportive friend who was worried about Freddie's wellbeing after such a dreadful shock.

Matt had seen Rosie's appraisal of him and she quickly averted her eyes, but not before she saw him smirk. She rolled her eyes, but couldn't prevent a whoosh of heat flushing into her cheeks, nor the fizzle of something she hadn't experienced for a while in her lower abdomen. She was surprised at the strength of her reaction. Was she attracted to Matt Wilson?

Chapter 10

Monday at the Windmill Café was unusually busy and by the time 6.30 came around Rosie's feet were screaming their objection to the unexpected onslaught, yet despite her tiredness and the worrying events of the previous day, she was much less anxious. That's what working in the café alongside Mia, and chatting to their loyal customers, did to her and she sent up her daily missive of gratitude to her director of fate for guiding her to Willerby, even if her stay at the village proved to be shorter than she would have liked.

She locked the door and turned to survey the room. The circular café, with its French windows opening onto the terrace beyond, still exuded an aroma of warm buttered scones, along with the fragrance of the sweet peas she had arranged for the tables and a faint hint of Flash. A smile tugged at her lips and she knew that a good session of scrubbing would chase away the aches and pains. As she worked her way from the countertops to the whitewashed wooden tables and then the floor, her spirits lifted.

When she had left London, with her heart cracked into multiple pieces, she had never dared to hope that she could make her life somewhere else, or that the life she pursued could be as happy – until recent events of course. She would even go as far as to admit that she was happier in Norfolk than she had been in the metropolis. For too long she had allowed her grief over the sudden ending of her relationship with Harry to marinate in a mixture of anger and self-pity. But no more. Her soul-baring to Matt the previous day had perforated her sadness and she could now say, hand on heart, that she could work towards viewing the anguish Harry had caused her as a mere blip on the landscape of her life.

Satisfied that the café and its kitchen were squeaky clean, and still relishing the delicate tang of fresh disinfection in her nostrils, she climbed the spiral stairs up to her studio. Then, something else occurred to her. Whilst she was on the subject of self-improvement, perhaps another thing she should work on was her obsession with orderliness. Would the world really fall apart if her shirts weren't folded in the same way or the café's spice jars weren't stored in alphabetical order or didn't have their labels facing the front?

She stripped and stepped into the shower, lathering her body and hair in beautiful, clean soapy bubbles using the Jo Malone toiletries Georgina had bought her for her birthday in July. Bliss!

Whilst she performed a valiant attempt to tame her curls, a crystal-clear image of her younger sister sprang into her mind. Georgina had championed every tiny footstep of her success, from graduating from catering college, to designing stunning or quirky bouquets for demanding brides, to baking twists on the humble fruit scone – she had even started to hint that it was time Rosie started dating again after the debacle with Harry. But she wasn't quite ready for that yet. The cadence of her life to date had been a symphony punctuated with tantalizing peaks and soul-scouring troughs. She needed a period of calm – or that was what she had told her persistent sister.

The success of the Windmill Café summer garden party had been a milestone, though. She had proved to herself that she could smile and laugh and live life to the full like everyone else. The armour plate she had erected around her heart was corroding with each passing week and she could now delve into her memories and extract a happier image than her previous go-to nightmare scenarios; her life was no longer filled with Bleeding Heart flowers – or *Dicentra Spectabilis* as Harry had insisted on calling them in the hope of catching her out. Nevertheless, even with Georgina's encouragement, it would be a while before she moved on to Kiss Me Over The Garden Gate – *Persicaria orientale*!

As Rosie brushed her teeth, Mia popped into her mind and a wide smile stretched her cheeks. She knew she had hit the friendship jackpot when Mia had walked into the café and strapped on one of her outrageous aprons, ready to bake up a storm. At the ripe old age of twenty-three, she was a natural baker, but that was probably down to the fact that her mother, Sarah, one of Carole's best friends, was a food tech teacher at the local High School. Rosie had loved the alcohol-infused nights they'd spent together putting the world to rights with that trio of oestrogen solace – chocolate, wine and gossip.

Was all this progress at an end? Would the café be forced

to shut its doors because of her? She hadn't heard anything further from Dr Bairstow, and she had been grateful for the hustle and bustle of the day because it had kept the churning trepidation at bay. However, now she was alone in her flat, she was finding it difficult not to allow the anxiety demons free rein. Where would she go next? And would she get another job in the catering industry if she was forced to leave under a cloud?

Rosie pulled on a new pair of jeans and her musings continued to meander around her brain. Inevitably, her thoughts drifted to Matt and how she had felt comfortable enough in his company to share the tragic details of her past relationship fiasco with him the previous day. Then, for some reason known only to her subconscious, she found herself imagining what he would look like without the black T-shirt that moulded his body like a second skin.

Okay, Rosie, she chastised herself, *get a grip!*

She tossed her hair brush onto the glass shelf beneath the mirror and selected a powder-blue tank top from her carefully co-ordinated wardrobe. Matt was much more than the local Bear Grylls, with an affinity for the great outdoors and a penchant for flying through the air on a zip wire. Even before he knew the results of Suki's tests, he had stood loyally by her side and come up with a practical solution to absolve her of guilt.

In a strange twist of fate, Matt had happened on one of the interests she had hoped to pursue in happier times before her childhood had imploded. Whilst she had loved her mother dearly, she had always been a Daddy's Girl. She had not only shared her father's passion for gardening, but also his obsession with detective novels, their favourites being the stories written by that grand dame of murder mysteries, Agatha Christie. She had read every one of her books before the age of fourteen and had loved discussing the twists and turns with him, especially enjoying their competitions to be the first to identify the culprit.

In fact, her interest in solving puzzles had fuelled her early ambitions to follow in her father's footsteps into the legal profession, albeit not into commercial law like him, but criminal defence. She had moved on from Agatha Christie to become fascinated with courtroom dramas, discovering John Grisham whose stories had sealed her dream to qualify as a lawyer. Sadly, she had been forced to shelve her best-laid plans in the face of overwhelming upheaval which had a detrimental effect on her exam results. Reading Law at university was no longer an option and she had been guided by a sympathetic personal tutor to her second passion, food, or more precisely, baking. In any case, passion or not, it was a talent she'd had no alternative but to hone if what was left of her devastated family were to eat.

Now she couldn't wait to take her place right there next to Matt, eager to ask questions, to weigh up the answers against the facts and discover the reasons why Suki became so ill so quickly. The irony was, at the moment, she seemed to be the suspect and not the protagonist sleuth! She would have given her precious Gaggia coffee machine to know what her beloved father would have said about that!

A sharp knock on the door of the café made her jump. She

secured her hair with a gem-encrusted comb, squared her shoulders and trotted down the stairs, with the precise where-abouts of the kitchen knives and rolling pin running through her mind. She rolled her eyes at her foolishness.

'Hi, Matt. Come in.'

'Actually, I thought you might want to take a walk over to Suki's lodge. I've just seen Dr Bairstow's Range Rover arrive in the car park. I think he's got the results of her blood tests.'

Rosie's spirits took a nosedive and her stomach felt as though she had plunged from the top of a rollercoaster down to the bottom. Nevertheless, the sooner she knew what had caused Suki's illness the better, even if she was to blame. She nodded and went to snatch her jacket from the coat stand, careful to lock the door behind her. As they made their way across the field to the lodges, apprehension clouded her thoughts and she struggled to make conversation but she knew Matt understood the reason for her silence.

Matt's rap on the door was answered by a white-faced William. Every eye in the room turned to see who had arrived, but no one objected to their presence. With tremendous effort, Rosie forced herself to ignore the nerves tingling at her finger-tips and to concentrate on what the doctor was saying to Suki and Felix. If she was going to be leaving Willerby, then she needed to understand the reasons why.

'So, the test results are conclusive – Suki was poisoned. However, it is extremely unlikely that the cause was linked to any of the food or drink served at the Windmill Café summer garden party.'

It took a few moments for what Dr Bairstow had said to

sink in. When it did, Rosie experienced such a surge of relief that she grabbed hold of Matt's hand to prevent herself from collapsing in a heap on the floor – she didn't want to give the doctor more work than he had bargained for. Inevitably, the conclusion raised a disturbing question.

'Do you mean... are you saying... that someone actually targeted me? That they put poison in my food or my drink at the party?' gasped Suki, her eyes widening in shock.

'I'm sorry to say that it looks like that's the case,' said Dr Bairstow.

The terror written across Suki's expression turned Rosie's stomach and for a brief moment she actually wanted the results of the test to have confirmed food poisoning. Whilst that conclusion would have been devastating for her, and for the future of the Windmill Café, these things happened in the catering industry. Yes, she would have lost her job, and Graham would have lost a great deal of money, but in all likelihood the business would probably have recovered from the ashes of its devastation. But now it looked like Matt's suspicions had come to fruition. Someone *had* wanted to hurt Suki – or worse – and a slither of fear meandered down her spine causing the hackles at her hairline to rise.

For several interminable minutes, no one spoke and silence rolled into every corner of the lodge. No one wanted to be the one to burst the bubble of calm-before-the-storm, as if by doing so the evil that may be loitering in their midst would be invited in. Suki, Jess, and Nadia sat huddled together on the leather sofa, their hands clutching the mugs of coffee they had been drinking when the doctor arrived to deliver the dreadful news. Felix stood next to the French doors leading to the veranda, his arms folded across his chest, staring out at the bucolic beauty of the Windmill Café's grounds. He lit a cigarette and it seemed no one had the heart or the energy to challenge him.

Rosie was glad she was holding Matt's hand as question after question coiled through her brain as if on a ribbon of tickertape. What if they hadn't found Suki when they did? How had the poison been administered? Who would do such a dreadful thing? And more to the point, why?

'Dr Bairstow, I noticed you removed a champagne bottle from the lodge,' said Matt, his voice sounding far too loud in the wood-panelled room. 'I assume that's because you believed it was the last thing Suki consumed and intended to check out the contents?'

'I have had the bottle checked...'

'Does that mean there *was* something in the champagne?' interrupted Lucas, running his fingers through his quiff which, despite all the recent turmoil, remained fixed in place at his forehead. Rosie did notice, however, that his eyes were rimmed with red and his previous boyish energy had melted away.

'So, does that mean that guy was poisoned too?' asked Nadia, flicking her eyes at Suki.

'What guy?' demanded Felix, drawing in a long drag of nicotine and allowing the smoke to escape from his lips in a mist of grey vapour. 'What are you talking about, Nadia? Suki? What's she talking about?'

Felix abandoned his place at the window and strode over

to where Suki and Nadia sat, his hands on his hips, glaring down at them. Nadia stared back at him, unwilling to go any further. Suki's face couldn't have bleached any whiter.

'What guy? Tell me!'

'Well, if you'd been here when you promised, you would know what I'm talking about, *and*, maybe none of this would have happened,' snapped Nadia. 'If you cared about Suki, really cared about her, instead of just her fame and potential fortune, you would have been at the garden party with us instead of getting plastered with your friends in Colchester. If you had been here, Suki would never have flounced off with that outward-bounds guy and we could all have been spared this nightmare!'

'What outward-bounds guy? Suki, what's Nadia wittering on about?' Felix's face was a mask of confusion as he swung his eyes to Lucas, then William, and finally bellowed, 'Will someone just tell me what's going on?'

It seemed Lucas was the only one prepared to put him out of his misery. 'One of the guys from the outward-bound centre in the village was at the garden party – Freddie something. Doesn't he work with you, Matt? Anyway, Suki took a bit of a shine to him, that's all.'

'That's all? That's all? So why did Nadia think he might have been poisoned if Suki had?'

Now everyone in the room squirmed. Even Lucas looked uncomfortable.

'Will? Lucas?'

'Sorry, mate...'

'It's okay,' interrupted Suki, raising her gaze to meet Felix's squarely. 'Felix, you weren't here. I knew you'd be getting drunk with the lads and I was angry with you. I'd had a couple of bottles of champagne and I decided to whip up the gossip mill. Freddie and I came back here to have a drink and talk music together.'

'You came back to *our* lodge with some random stranger?'

'Felix, I get to decide who I spend my time with, not you...'

'What's the matter with you, Suki. If you were poisoned deliberately, the person most likely to be responsible is this Freddie guy. I want him found and I want him arrested. In fact, I'm calling the police. This is turning into something much more serious than an innocent bout of food poisoning.'

'Before you do that, Felix, perhaps you would permit me to finish answering Matt's question,' said Dr Bairstow, raising his eyebrows which only served to highlight the crooked bridge of his nose. 'Whilst the lab found no trace of any toxic substance in the champagne bottle, they did detect traces of a foreign substance capable of causing nausea and vomiting in the bottle containing Suki's throat spray.'

A gasp of disbelief reverberated around the room.

'Oh, my God! I knew it,' cried Felix. 'You and your bloody throat spray. I knew it would make you sick one day. Why on earth you persist in using it all the time is beyond me. Maybe now you'll listen to me for once and ditch it. There's no reason why you can't just go on stage and sing without relying on contaminated comforters made from dodgy stuff you buy over the internet.'

'The lab has promised to expedite their efforts to identify the precise ingredient that caused your illness, Suki, and as soon as I have that information, I'll call you. In the meantime, perhaps you should refrain from using it again.'

'I will, Doctor, and thank you for coming over here in person to tell me about the results.' Suki gave him a weak smile of gratitude before attempting to push herself up from the chair, clearly still feeling the after-effects of her recent stomach-emptying trauma.

'It's okay, Suki. I can see myself out.'

Dr Bairstow retrieved his medical bag, smiled at Matt and Rosie and left.

'Felix, I think you need to apologize to Matt,' said Suki.

'What for?'

'For labelling his friend Freddie a criminal.'

Felix flashed his eyes at Matt and muttered something that was definitely not an apology under his breath.

'I'm sorry, everyone, but I really would like to have an early night. I'm absolutely exhausted, but tomorrow is another day in sunny Norfolk and I for one am looking forward to getting this holiday back on track. I promise not to sing or to use any throat spray!'

'Are you sure we're going to be safe?' asked Jess, jumping up to grab her sister's arm. 'What if there's a murderer around? What if they try again? What if I'm next on their list. You can't leave me here!'

Rosie saw that Jess's face was suffused with genuine panic. All evening she'd had the appearance of a forlorn toddler who had just been informed she had been left off the birthday party guest list and Rosie wouldn't have been surprised if she had stuck her thumb in her mouth and indulged in a sulk.

'You'll be fine, Jess darling. There's no reason to suspect this was anything other than an unfortunate accident. And, anyway, you have Lucas to take care of you.'

'Oh my God! I'm definitely going to die!'

Chapter 11

The next morning dawned overcast and it seemed the summer heatwave had broken. Heavy, bulbous clouds sporting bruised underbellies drifted in from the sea and grazed the canopy of trees in whose depths Ultimate Adventures was located, yet the weather reflected Rosie's mood.

When she'd got back to her flat the previous night it had been after midnight and, for the first time since arriving at the Windmill Café, she hadn't felt the insistent pull to give the surfaces one last wipe down with the anti-bacterial spray before she retired to bed – she had just been too exhausted. However, her tiredness was nothing compared to her relief that the café had been exonerated and would live to serve its customers freshly buttered scones for another day. She had drifted off to sleep as soon as her head had hit the pillow.

Nevertheless, she had woken up at three in the morning with a jolt of alarm. Within minutes her body was covered in a hot sweat of panic as a kaleidoscope of new worries rampaged through her head.

How could she have forgotten? Hadn't Suki sourced the contents of her throat spray, well, the Jarrah honey at least, from her own store cupboard in the Windmill Café? Should she tell Matt? Maybe he would be delighted to resume his amateur sleuthing when she confessed that Suki had not acquired a contaminated batch of her spray from the internet.

Rosie had tossed and turned until her alarm clock told her it was 7 a.m., then padded down the staircase to survey the café kitchen, fingering her mobile phone as she considered whether to call Matt and confess to a new twist in the ongoing saga. She rummaged in the cupboard and found a second jar of the Jarrah honey that her sister had bought her for her birthday. She scrutinized the label and, whilst she was certain that Harrods would never sell contaminated honey, there was only one way to find out. She unscrewed the lid and before she could think too much about what she was doing, she tasted the honey and waited.

Nothing happened.

After thirty minutes, she hadn't rushed to the bathroom or felt any ill-effects whatsoever and she concluded that it must have been one of the other ingredients in Suki's throat spray that was the culprit. She let out a long, ragged sigh, before being jerked out of her trace by a rap on the door.

'Hello? Is it okay to come in? I know the café doesn't open until eleven. If I'm disturbing you I can come back later?'

'Oh, hi, Suki. No, no, of course you're not disturbing me. How are you feeling today?'

'A little woozy still, but otherwise I'm fine. I just need to get away from Felix for a few hours. He's driving me crazy.

I'm afraid he's still fixated with involving the authorities, and all William wants us to do is leave. I want to stay until Dr Bairstow gets back to me about what kind of "foreign substance" was in my spray, so I've told Felix and William that they can do whatever they like but I'm not going anywhere. I know my illness has nothing to do with the Windmill Café. I love it here, it's so restful. Actually, Rosie, I wanted to ask you and Mia a favour.'

'Of course, ask away.'

'Would you be up for giving me, Jess and Nadia a lesson in how to make a batch of those delicious Stilton and grape scones we had at the garden party? And, if we have time, maybe we could also bake some of your pineapple and coconut cookies?'

Rosie stared at Suki, totally surprised at her request. Surely the last thing she would want to do after what had happened to her was indulge in a full-blown bake-a-thon.

'Are you sure?'

'What Rosie actually means is that she and Mia would be delighted to showcase a few of the Windmill Café's signature bakes,' laughed Matt appearing on the doorstep of the café, waving a handful of white confectionery bags in the air. 'I thought you'd appreciate breakfast, why don't you stick the kettle on while I give Mia a call to see if she can start her shift a little earlier?'

'Oh, erm, yes, thank you, Matt. Sorry, Suki, I'd love to do that for you, but we'd better get started right away because there's only two hours until the café opens to the public.'

'Great! I'll pay you for your time and all the extra ingredients.'

'Oh, no, that won't be...'

'I want to. I'm thinking, with your permission of course, of having a cake sale in the car park for the local children's music and drama school that Carole told me about at the garden party on Sunday. What do you think?'

'I think it's a lovely idea,' smiled Rosie, leading Suki into the kitchen, her spirits soaring as they invariably did whenever she was about to treat herself to a morning of unbridled culinary fun. Scones and cookies were amongst the simplest of recipes to create and she knew the kitchen was cleaner than it had ever been. What could go wrong?

'I'll leave these croissants here and catch up with you later, Rosie. Have fun!'

Matt leaned forward to deposit a farewell kiss on Rosie's cheek. His gesture was so unexpected she drew back in surprise and stumbled into the work bench. He laughed, shook his head, and strode from the terrace as her face flooded with heat once again.

'He's gorgeous. You are a *very* lucky girl!' smiled Suki, standing next to Rosie with her hands on her slender hips as she surveyed Matt's retreating figure.

'Oh, no, we're not... I mean, Matt and I are just friends.'

'Didn't look like it from where I was standing!' giggled Jess who had joined them with Lucas in tow. 'If I didn't have my incredibly handsome Lucas to keep me warm at night, you'd have to fight me off with your spatula, Rosie!'

Rosie was shocked to discover how flustered she was at their teasing. She was surprised that others had noticed the chemistry between her and Matt. Although she had denied it, she had to admit they were right – there was a definite buzz of electricity in the air whenever Matt Wilson was in the vicinity. She had no idea what it meant, nor did she understand it.

Hadn't she declared herself finished with all romantic relationships? Didn't they all end in disaster one way or another? Even though she had moved on, she could still recall the sharpness of the pain she had endured when she had broken up with Harry, especially after the way she'd discovered his infidelity, and there was no way she was going there again.

'Okay. Everyone help themselves to one of our Windmill Café aprons and we'll get started on the scones.'

'At last, Nadia! Where have you been?'

'Don't nag. Anyway, aren't we supposed to be on holiday? Why should we be forced to get up at the crack of dawn?'

'Oooh, someone didn't get any act...shun in the bedroom department last night!'

Lucas grinned with mischief at Nadia's reaction as he sprinkled flour through a sieve into a silver bowl from a great height. A good handful fell onto the floor and Rosie almost had a coronary. It took all her willpower not to crouch down and wipe it up straight away. She wasn't sure she was cut out to be a cookery teacher and she kept checking her watch, hoping that Mia would arrive before she attacked Lucas with the meat cleaver for leaving snail-trails of desiccated coconut on her precious units. Never mind a poisoning for Matt to solve, there would be a murder!

'When you make scones, it's essential to make sure all

the ingredients are cold and that you don't overwork the mixture,' said Rosie, tossing in a generous portion of crumbled Stilton.

'Hey, Jess, do you think I could persuade my boss Marcus to offer a selection of fruit and savoury scones to his customers?'

'I don't think San Antonio is ready for scones, Lucas darling, but maybe these cookies could work,' Suki laughed.

'I don't know why you still work in that flea-pit of a place,' said Nadia.

'Needs must, Nad. We haven't all got a private income to rely on,' Lucas said, glancing across at Suki from beneath his eyelashes.

Even in the humidity of the café kitchen, with the oven on full-blast as their scones produced the most delicious smell of melting cheese, Lucas's blond quiff stayed rigidly in place. He had pushed the sleeves of his shirt up to his elbows to reveal a scattering of fair hairs across his forearms. Rosie couldn't help but smile when she realized that, in the right light, Lucas really could be mistaken for his hero, Jamie Oliver.

'Hi everyone. I hope I haven't missed out on all the fun?'

'Hi, Mia.' Rosie gave her friend a hug of welcome before whispering in her ear. 'Am I glad you're here. I just need you to channel some of your mum's fabulous cookery presentation skills and I think we'll be fine.'

'No problem, you can definitely count on me.'

Mia grabbed one of her signature aprons from a drawer, this one made from the same fabric as the green wide-legged culottes she was wearing, and fastened the strings around her waist. She looked like an advertisement for an over-decorated Christmas tree.

'Okay, everyone, Mia is going to talk you through the recipe for the pineapple and coconut cookies whilst I make a start on the tidying up.'

Rosie surveyed the kitchen and cringed. Goose bumps rippled around her body as she struggled with an almost overwhelming urge to shove every one of the guests out of the room so she could get on with washing down all the surfaces with soapy water. She knew she was being unreasonable. She knew it was something she should consider getting professional help with – but what was the point when she also knew exactly where her problem stemmed from and why it had raised its ugly head recently?

'Mmm, this chocolate is delicious!' declared Jess, shoving a handful of white chocolate buttons into her cheeks and pulling a comical face at her sister like an over-stuffed hamster.

'You're not supposed to eat the ingredients before the cookies are even baked!'

'You talking to me?' Jess said in a gangster-type voice before bursting into hysterical laughter and sending splinters of chocolate everywhere.

Rosie turned her back and busied herself with filling a bucket with scalding hot water and adding her best friend – a generous slug of disinfectant. Her chest felt as though it was going to burst as she tried to keep a lid on her churning emotions. Why, oh why, had she agreed to give Suki and her messy friends a cookery lesson?

'Wow, these scones look amazing! Is it okay if we sample our masterpieces, Rosie?'

'Of course. There's butter in the fridge for the scones.'

The kitchen filled with the most delicious fragrance of warm caramel as the cookies were removed from the oven and transferred to a wire rack to cool. Rosie made a cafetière of coffee and everyone moved to the terrace to indulge in the products of their labour, laughing and chatting about their life in Ibiza and how different things would be when Suki started touring to promote her album. Rosie relaxed, relieved that the tutorial was over and she had her precious kitchen back under her control.

'Ah, so this is where you've all disappeared to?' said Felix, snatching up a cookie and taking a bite.

'I see you're happy to eat at the Windmill Café, then?' observed Suki, watching Felix's expression closely.

Clearly Felix hadn't thought his actions through properly because he stopped in his tracks, his mouth full of warm cookie, his eyes widened with surprise. Rosie suspected that he was in the process of considering the etiquette of spitting out the offending biscuit and reluctantly thinking better of it. He swallowed and paused as everyone waited for his verdict. It was apparent from the look on Felix's face that he was expecting to keel over in agony.

'Well?' demanded Jess.

'Before you answer my sister's question, you might like to know that I made these cookies with my own fair hands!' cried Suki.

'They're very... erm, well, nice.'

'Nice? Is that the best you can do? I've spent the last two hours slaving in a hot kitchen and all you can say is "they're nice"?'

'Delicious, amazing, magnificent! What do you want me to say, Suke?'

'As my boyfriend I expect you to show an interest in what I'm doing. It wouldn't have killed you to have joined us this morning. I booked this break so we could spend time together but so far you've chosen to spend all your time either drinking with your friends or asleep.'

'I wasn't asleep. I was busy on the phone making enquiries!'

'Enquiries? What sort of enquiries?'

'I've managed to speak to the environmental health guys responsible for this area and they've promised to come over as soon as the lab tells us what kind of poison they found in your spray.'

'You've done what?' cried Suki, shooting an apologetic glance at Rosie and Mia. 'Felix, you really are a complete moron. The reason we've just spent the whole morning baking is so that we have a selection of baked goods to sell to the café's visitors. I was going to donate the profits to a local kid's drama club. How can I do that when you've arranged for a bunch of inspectors to come swarming all over the place? I want you to cancel them right away.'

Felix held Suki's eyes for a moment, clearly wanting to argue back, but realizing he had an audience who were likely to maul him to pieces if he tried, he spun on his hand-made Italian leather loafers and left the café.

'Felix really is an absolute... oh, God, who's this ringing?'

Suki scrambled around in her Birkin for her phone, checking the caller ID before swiping her finger across the screen and walking out onto the terrace to take her call in private.

'Hello, Dr Bairstow? Yes, thanks for calling. So, what did the lab say?'

Chapter 12

Rosie noticed that Suki's face was devoid of its usual colour again, and that she was fiddling with her hair like her sister Jess did, wrapping a coil around her thumb and index finger in agitation. It was obvious that what Dr Bairstow was telling Suki wasn't good news and her stomach lurched like a penny down a well as she wondered what new horror he had delivered. She didn't have to wait too long for the hammer to fall.

'Oh my God, Oh my God! Oh my God!'

Suki dropped down on one of the café's overstuffed sofas and burst into tears.

'What's happened? Who was that on the phone?' asked Jess as she rushed over to curl her arm around her sister's shoulders.

'It was Dr Bairstow. The lab has identified the "foreign substance" that was found in my throat spray. It was something called aconitine. Apparently, I've been *lucky*! In larger doses it can affect the cardiovascular system and cause multiple organ failure but because I only ingested a small amount and I was sick almost straight away, there were no long-lasting effects. Oh my God, what if...'

Rosie stared mutely at Suki, her jaw loose, her brain sending out synapses like fireworks as she tried to comprehend what Dr Bairstow's findings meant. What on earth was aconitine and how had it got into Suki's throat spray? Far from matters at the Windmill Café improving, they were getting worse, much worse, and Suki was clearly scared at hearing of this turn of events.

'What the hell is aconitine?' demanded Felix, reappearing at the French doors along with a cloud of cigarette smoke, and taking a seat on the other side of Suki. He reached into his pocket and handed her a bunch of tissues to dry her tears, the tremble in his hands belying his concern.

'Dr Bairstow hadn't heard of it either, so he did some digging on the internet. He found this case a couple of years ago – a gardener found dead in his garden and doctors couldn't find out why. It was eventually discovered to be aconitine poisoning from a plant called devil's helmet or monkshood – apparently one of the deadliest flowers in the plant kingdom. He's promised to email me the case and photographs of the plant, although I'm not sure I want him to.'

'But, Suki, how could you have come into contact with monkshood?' asked Rosie, her brain starting to clear as she wrestled with the implications of this new turn of events.

'I have no idea, but Dr Bairstow's had to inform the authorities and they're sending over a team of inspectors to investigate sometime tomorrow. Rosie, I'm sorry, but you'll have to close the café until they've given the place the all-clear and we've been asked to stay until it's over in case they want to ask us any questions.'

'Gosh, Suki, it should be me apologizing to you. This is the last thing you deserve when all you wanted was a relaxing break. I'll do whatever the authorities want; close the café, the holiday site, anything. I want to get to the bottom of this as much as anyone.'

'But if it was in Suki's throat spray, it's unlikely anyone else came into contact with that, don't you think?' said Mia, speaking for the first time since Suki's phone call.

Suki's eyes widened as if realizing something for the first time. Her tears returned with a vengeance and her voice rose up an octave to squeak level.

'Oh my God, you're right! How did the aconitine poison get in my throat spray bottle? Do you think someone put it there? Do you think someone wanted to hurt me... to kill me?' Suki crumbled into huge wracking sobs and she rocked backwards and forwards in Jess and Felix's arms as Nadia looked on in mute desperation and horror.

A roll of nausea swept through Rosie as she tried to comprehend what Suki had just said. If Suki's suspicions turned out to be right, who could have done such a terrible thing? And more to the point, why? Had they wanted to damage Suki's voice so she couldn't sing for them that evening or was it something darker altogether? And why use such an unusual method? If Suki had been poisoned with bleach, then that would have been a different story, but whatever Felix thought of her café, she was one hundred percent certain that there was no monkshood stored in her kitchen cupboards!

Then an agonizing bolt of electricity shot through her heart – could it have been in the honey? The jar had been sealed when she'd handed it over to Suki, she'd checked, so how had it got there? It was no good, Rosie couldn't hang onto her emotions any longer and tears trickled down her cheeks. She had to say something.

'Suki, do you think... do you think it could have been the honey I gave you? Remember, you came to the café to ask if I had any honey because you'd run out? Did you use it to make your spray?'

Suki's eyes, red-rimmed and bloodshot met Rosie's, but as usual before she could utter a word, Felix had leapt from his seat and was straight in there.

'I told you this place is a death trap! It's just as well the doctor's informed the authorities and the café is going to be shut down! I'm going back to the lodge to make sure no one touches that honey before the inspectors arrive and I'll insist that they test it right away.'

Felix stormed out of the café, shoving a recently arrived William roughly out of his way, and the others followed him.

'Hey, guys, what's going on? Suki?'

Rosie saw something more than concern for Suki's wellbeing in William's eyes, and had her world not been crumbling down around her she would have dissected its meaning further. However, she had much more pressing things on her mind.

'Mia, can you help me to make a "Closed" sign for the front gate?'

'Sure.'

When they had finished hanging the hand-made sign on the car park fence, Rosie gathered together a basket of things to take upstairs to her flat. She didn't want to interrupt the investigation once it started, and she certainly had no intention of watching whilst they tore her beloved little café apart. A cauldron of dread churned in her stomach, but she knew that was nothing compared to how Suki must be feeling. The poor girl could have died and there was the added possibility that someone had targeted her! Oh God, she thought, what if the assailant was still lurking around in the holiday site? She dropped her basket and ran to the bathroom.

'Rosie? Are you okay?' called Mia, her voice tight with anxiety.

'Erm...'

'Look, I want you to come and stay with me. That way the inspectors can do what they want without you having to be there. Why don't you go upstairs, pack a bag and we'll leave them to it? No arguments.'

Rosie peered round the door at her friend and the sympathy on her face nearly sent her into another deluge of tears, but she managed to hang on.

'Mia, I would love to do that, but with Graham out of the country, the café's my responsibility. I need to stay here.'

'Well, nothing will be happening until tomorrow, so let's get away for a few hours.'

'Okay.'

Rosie gave Mia a weak smile of gratitude, slung a few random items into her handbag and locked the café before joining Mia next to her little cream Fiat 500 in the car park. She couldn't wait to escape. If she stayed, all she would be able to think about would be the inspectors combing through her kitchen, moving everything from its allocated space, testing every nook and cranny – no matter how certain she was that they wouldn't find a speck of dirt or molecule of germs anywhere, she was still terrified of their impending visit.

'I've been thinking,' mused Mia as she steered round the narrow roads towards the converted barn she shared with her parents. 'It could be nothing, but...'

'What?'

'Well, no, nothing...'

'Mia?'

'It's just Suki told me that she and Nadia went for a walk through the woodland on Sunday morning before the party. Could she have accidentally touched or brushed against the petals of one of these monkshood flowers?'

'It's not touching that causes illness. It's ingesting.'

'Well, I know exactly who we should ask about poisonous plants.'

'Who?'

'Freddie.'

'Why Freddie?'

'Don't you remember he told you at the garden party that whilst you might be the go-to girl for bridal flowers, he was the man when it came to wild flowers? Why don't we take a detour over to the outward-bound centre and ask him what he knows? We can talk to Matt about the inspection too. He'll know how to handle it until Graham gets back. I can't wait to see Matt's face when we tell him that his super-sleuthing skills are back in demand. Unlike you, I'm confident the inspectors won't find anything wrong with that honey you gave Suki – it came from Harrods for God's sake! No, if you want my opinion, Suki was spot on. Someone put something in her spray. What we need to find out is who.'

'I think you're right – and it has to be someone who knows Suki uses her spray before every concert not just to help her voice but because it calms her stage nerves. I could be wrong but I reckon that poison was put in her bottle and the poisoner didn't expect her to use it here in Willerby but when she got back home to Ibiza. And if I'm right, the only people on my list who could have done that are the people in her party, the people she calls her friends. If we want to save the café, then it's up to us, and Matt, to find out who.'

'And why!'

'Yes, and why.'

A surge of optimism sliced through Rosie's veins. Instead of her previous go-to reaction of running away from the misfortunes life threw at her, she was choosing to take a more positive stance and it felt good to be doing something to salvage the café's reputation, as well as her own. She was absolutely determined to do everything she could to preserve the reputation of her beloved café by finding out what was going on – and there would be the added benefit of making her father proud.

Chapter 13

As they drove to the other side of the village, Rosie rolled down the window of Mia's little Fiat to marvel at the beauty of its landscaped gardens. All the lawns had been meticulously trimmed, rectangles of green velvet rippling in the breeze like liquid luck, some strewn with the tiny white dots of daisies, some as perfect as bowling greens. In every garden, the herbaceous borders burst with geraniums, hollyhocks and delphinium, vivid with summer bounty. A parade of pansies and petunias, marigolds and alyssum skirted the flower beds, flanked by sturdy rhododendron bushes, magnolias and wooden arches clad in clematis, all in full flower. Birdsong echoed through the tangled branches of the oak and horse chestnut trees to the accompaniment of the languid drone of a solitary lawn mower.

A waft of fragrance floated through the open car window. For Rosie, the sweet aroma of crushed rose petals was the scent of summer more than any other floral bouquet. She wished with all her heart that she could retreat to a shady bench amongst the blooms, with one of her favourite glossy cookery books, and lose herself in another world.

'It's really pretty, isn't it?' said Mia, sending a smile in Rosie's direction. 'Willerby has won best village in the Britain in Bloom competition quite a few times. Hey, Rosie, your flower arrangements at the garden party were amazing, have you ever thought of entering any competitions? You'd get my vote!'

'Thanks, Mia. Actually, I've won quite a few prizes already.'

'You have? Why've you kept that a secret? Is it because Carole might co-opt you onto the church rota?'

Rosie laughed, but the familiar feeling of discomfort started to rotate around her abdomen. Looking back, she knew that entering her floral art into competitions had been the beginning of the end for her and Harry's relationship. Things had never quite been the same after she had won a prestigious gold medal at a floristry competition for which Harry had spent weeks creating his own submission, sourcing exotic flowers from the far side of the globe and declaring his design to be a shoo-in. Especially as he had spent the days leading up to the judging disparaging every aspect of her arrangement and advising her on how to bring it up to a more professional standard.

'Of course not. I'm proud of my achievements, it's just that... well... Harry was jealous of the accolades so I just got used to not singing about them from the rooftops, that's all.'

'That man has a lot to answer for!'

'True. You know, I'll never forget the look of complete incredulity on his face the very first time I entered a flower arranging contest and my name was announced as the winner in the "most innovative bridal bouquet" category. We had our first big row on the way home, but from that day onwards, I got a taste for entering my work into competitions.'

'So what kind of things did you win?' laughed Mia. 'A lorryload of manure?'

'Not quite, but you're not too far off. I've won a few garden forks, a lawn mower – very useful when you live in a tiny flat in inner London. Oh, and let's not forget the year's supply of slug pellets. But my favourite prize was a VIP trip for two to the spa at The Langham for a design I presented in an over-sized cocktail glass. Of course, Harry was in a sulk because he didn't win with his magnolias, and he refused to come with me, so I took my sister, Georgie. When I got back all scrubbed and fragrant, Harry was surprisingly contrite and like a fool I thought it was because he had missed me. I should have known better because it was the following week that I found him with Heidi.'

'Rosie, I'm so sorry you had to go through that.'

The image of Harry and Heidi together floated across her vision, but the memory was too painful to dwell on and she was grateful when they crunched into the car park of the outward-bound activity centre.

Matt answered the door of the huge wooden cabin that housed Ultimate Adventures' reception and office with an apple clenched between his teeth and surprise etched on his face. The tang of fried bacon drifted to Rosie's nostrils reminding her stomach that in the early morning baking frenzy she had foregone breakfast *and* lunch.

'Come in. Want a coffee?'

Perceptive as usual, thought Rosie. A small smile tugged at

her lips as she and Mia followed Matt into the tiny kitchen at the back of the lodge.

'So, to what do I owe the honour? Why aren't you at the café?'

Whilst Mia explained the reasons for their visit to Matt, Rosie glanced around the room and the desperation to create order that always lurked just beneath the surface was almost overwhelming. The whole room was a maelstrom of chaos. It was probably larger than the kitchen she worked in at the café, but because of the jumble of discarded cartons, packaging and plastic bottles on every available surface, it looked a lot smaller. The only space on the workbenches was an area next to the coffee machine where Matt was preparing their drinks. Every wall held either a noticeboard pinned with numerous flyers, or a whiteboard scrawled with instructions and schedules. If this was what the kitchen looked like, she would hate to see the state of Ultimate Adventures' office.

She slid into a chair at the pine table opposite Matt and gave him a smile, but she knew it didn't meet her eyes. Uncontrolled emotions churned through her body causing her to feel woozy as her mind wandered from the anxiety of the inspectors' imminent visit to the irresistible urge to start tidying up and scrubbing down the countertops. She surreptitiously pushed her hands under her bottom and started counting backwards from one hundred, matching each number with a long exhalation of breath.

She knew Matt was watching her discomfort and she had never been more relieved when she heard the crunch of tyres on gravel outside the kitchen window signalling that Freddie had arrived for his shift.

'I think I'll go and say hi to Freddie.'

Rosie couldn't get out of her seat fast enough and almost sprinted to the car park to wait for Freddie to unload the boot of his ancient air-force blue Land Rover and transport a huge box of ropes and crampons into the storage hut next to the reception.

'Hi, Rosie! Didn't expect to see you down here? Have you come to take a flight on the zip wire?'

'God, no thank you!'

A shiver flashed up her spine at the thought of climbing up the rickety rope ladder she could see dangling in the trees to her right. She squinted into the canopy of leaves overhead and could just about make out the wooden platform from where Ultimate Adventures' clients hurtled themselves into oblivion – willingly. She would rather spend an hour in Matt's kitchen!

'Perhaps something else, then? What about rock-climbing?' smiled Freddie, his open, friendly face nudging her spirits northwards. He had been through a nightmare over the last couple of days, but his sweet temperament was as upbeat as it had always been.

Rosie resolved to learn from Freddie's example so she pushed her shoulders back and inhaled a deep confidence-inducing breath. Maybe now *was* the time to learn something new? She cast another glance at the zip wire and cringed. She had been so focused on the sky-high obstacle course that she hadn't realized that Matt and Mia had joined them.

'Mia's brought me up to speed with her suspicions and I totally agree with her. We've got to investigate what's going on at the windmill's lodges ourselves. And you're spot on, Rosie, we need to find out more about Suki's friends' backgrounds. However, while I've got you here, you might as well check out one of our activities. It'll take your mind off what's going on at the café,' said Matt.

'What's going on at the café?' asked Freddie, his eyes suddenly taking on a hunted look.

Mia quickly filled Freddie in about the results of Suki's blood tests and the visit of the environmental health inspectors. 'We were wondering if you could tell us anything about monkshood?'

Freddie's mouth gaped. 'How could Suki have got something like that in her throat spray? I'm almost certain monkshood, or *aconitum napellus*, doesn't even grow in the woodlands around here. I've heard of it in other parts of the country but never here. It does have beautiful, deep blue-purple petals that resemble a monk's hood, hence the name, but it's also known as Devil's Helmet because it's so toxic.' Freddie ran his palms over his forearms; the copper-coloured hairs had risen into goose bumps. 'Are you absolutely sure that's what Dr Bairstow said?'

'Yes, sure.'

'Well, I think that's put me off suggesting wild flower tours alongside the clay-pigeon shooting.'

'Are there any other poisonous plants scattered around the woodland?' Rosie asked, keen to delay the moment when Matt handed her a safety helmet and hi-vis vest. 'There must be a few?'

'Oh, yes, there are several. There are the ones everyone's familiar with – laburnum, yew, foxgloves, even *convallaria majalis,* more commonly known as lily-of-the-valley. We have all those in Norfolk. Got to be careful with flowering plants – they're not just innocuous baubles to brighten up your garden. Rhubarb leaves are toxic and used to make rat poison and don't forget the daffodils, ubiquitous around here in the spring. The flowers are harmless but the bulbs and stems can cause severe stomach upsets. However, the most common plant that everyone knows is toxic is the Deadly Nightshade – *atropa belladonna* – the whole plant is lethal.'

'What about other rare species?'

Rosie knew all about the flowers she used to make wedding bouquets, wreaths and table decorations, but she realized that her knowledge of more toxic plants was not as detailed as Freddie's. He seemed to be an enthusiast and she tried not to think about what his interest in horticulture might mean as he warmed to his subject.

'There's been a recent escalation in gardeners growing wild flowers. TV programmes have encouraged people to sow wild flower seeds to encourage bees and wild animals into their gardens, so there's been a resurgence of plants we had thought were extinct. Now I come to think about it, there was a case a couple of years ago up the coast at Souter Lighthouse where the corncockle – *agrostemma githago* – was found. Every part of the plant is filled with glycoside githagin and agrostemmic acid, just a brush of the petals can cause severe stomach cramps, vomiting, diarrhoea, dizziness and, in extreme cases, death.'

Freddie was on a roll as his audience listened in fascination. He reminded Rosie of one of her old chemistry teachers, Mr Jarvis, who was so passionate about his subject that his cheeks used to glow when he regaled them with interesting science-related snippets.

'With modern farming methods and excessive use of chemical pesticides it was thought the corncockle had been wiped out, but it was once very common in the nineteenth century. In the Souter case, the experts thought it was possible that a seed had blown in from a garden where someone had cultivated the plant or, my own personal opinion, that it had lain dormant in the soil until the ground was disturbed.'

'Freddie, I really think it's a great idea to offer tours of the woodlands around here,' said Mia, her eyes sparkling with vicarious pride. 'In fact, why don't you take me for a stroll around the site now? I'd love to hear more.'

Rosie watched Mia link her arm through Freddie's and the pair sauntered off through the trees. She turned to smile at Matt but his eyes were glinting with mischief.

'Okay, Miss Barnes, time to fulfil your promise to give field archery a go. Don't look so terrified. I know you're going to love it!' Matt strode into the storeroom behind the office and came back with an armful of equipment. 'Here, put this on.'

Rosie took a flat piece of leather with three elastic fastenings from Matt and turned it over in her hand. She had no idea what to do with it. Not wanting to look like a complete idiot, she watched from beneath her eyelashes as he yanked his own protective arm brace onto the inside of his forearm and then copied him.

'Okay, here's your quiver. We'll start with six arrows each, I think.'

As Matt leaned forward to fasten the quiver securely around her waist, Rosie caught a whiff of his lemony cologne and smiled. Perhaps she was going to enjoy this activity if it meant being in such close contact with Action Man himself, she thought, until Matt produced the bow from its wooden case and her jaw gaped.

'Is that a long bow?'

'No. This is a recurve bow – see how the riser is moulded to the shape of your left hand? You balance the bow on the arch between your left thumb and index finger like this. The arrow is then placed on this rest and the nock at the end is clicked into the string like this. Make sure you're wearing your finger guard when you draw the string back, with the arrow between your first two fingers and your elbow and forearm horizontal to your cheek. Unbreakable rule number one – never draw the string unless you are aiming for a target. Ready to give it a go?'

'Erm...'

Rosie fumbled as she tried to take the bow from Matt's hand. If it wasn't for Matt's swift reactions the whole thing would have tumbled to the ground.

'Sorry.'

'Here, let me demonstrate.'

To Rosie's surprise, Matt moved behind her and pulled her spine into his abdomen so that she made contact with the rock-hard muscles of his torso. He then slid his left arm under hers, cupped her hand holding up the bow, draped his right arm over her shoulder and guided her fingers into the right position on the string. She could feel his breath tickling her right cheek and she was relieved that he couldn't see her face when he placed his chin on her shoulder and whispered. 'Pull the string back only as far as the corner of your lips before releasing the arrow.'

When Matt stepped back to allow her to aim at the first target – fastened to a tree trunk less than twenty metres away – she thought her whole body would crumple to the ground like a puppet clipped of its strings. However, she managed to stay upright and released the arrow, watching in dismay as it flew straight past the target and imbedded in a branch to her left. Rosie's heart leapt into her mouth as a bird gave flight with a loud shriek of objection to having his dinner interrupted.

'Great first attempt.'

'Really?'

'Yes. Now stand next to me and watch my stance. Your left arm should be stretched out at right angles to your body when balancing the bow, your right elbow should be raised and parallel, your head turned ninety degrees to your left. Look through the sight, line it up to the centre of the target and aim for the gold.'

Matt drew the string of his bow to his chin, lowered the arrow to the target and released the string. The arrow flew straight into the centre of the straw boss and he allowed the bow to see-saw forward on his thumb. Rosie was deeply impressed by the grace and elegance of the whole movement, not to mention the accuracy of the shot.

'Okay. Let's move on.'

Rosie almost cantered to the next target in the woodland in anticipation of another demonstration from Matt. He had been right – this was the perfect way to relax after the earlier trauma at the café.

'Why don't you take up your stance while I watch?'

Rosie tried to remember how Matt had held his bow. 'Like this?'

'Looks great. But try looking straight ahead first to get your posture right, then turning your head to the left, raising your bow in a smooth, uninterrupted movement, positioning the sight on the target...'

'But where's the target?'

Matt smiled. 'Right there.'

'But that's a... oh, I get it.'

As Rosie squinted through the shadowy light she could just about make out the silhouette of an over-large grey squirrel. On closer scrutiny, she realized it was made from straw and had a target attached to its tail. She took a steadying breath, followed Matt's instructions to the letter, and fired off her next arrow.

'Yay!' cried Rosie, as a surge of exhilaration whipped around her body.

'Congratulations, you made your first hit. I think you might be a natural.'

'That felt amazing! I really didn't think I would be able to do anything like this. It's obviously all down to my fabulous instructor! I bet everyone loves shooting in the woods with you.'

Again, Rosie's cheeks glowed as she realized she had made yet another risqué comment to Matt, but she had seen his eyes suddenly cloud over. The ragged, tormented look she had seen on his face as he'd argued with Mia outside the vicarage had returned.

'Well, not everyone.'

'What do you mean?'

Rosie desperately wanted Matt to open up about his past, to confide in her about what had happened at St Andrew's church to cause such sadness, such heartache. She spotted an upturned tree trunk and sat down, making it clear she was offering a listening ear just as he had done when she had told him about Harry.

Matt hesitated for a moment before joining her, clasping his hands between his thighs and lowering his head.

'I know you must have thought my reaction that night at the vicarage was strange. I also know that Mia won't have told you what was behind it because she and Freddie are such loyal friends. The truth is that I can't face even being in the vicinity of St Andrew's church, so it's easier to simply avoid the place altogether. Carole and Roger were so kind, so sympathetic, helpful and practical, and I'm grateful for everything they did to ease the hurt, but I never want to set foot in Carole's cosy kitchen again.'

Matt was silent for so long, lost in the labyrinth of painful memories, that Rosie thought he'd forgotten she was there. She wanted to ask him to explain, but she knew she had to let him find the right words in his own time. If she had thought this was going to be a straightforward archery shoot, a chance to simply deflect the anxiety over what was happening at the café, then she had got much more than she had bargained for. And yet she was glad they had this chance to spend time together. Sitting there, beneath the rippling canopy of leaves, she felt closer to Matt, as though he was more than just a friend intent on exposing her ineptitude for outdoor activities and she wanted to offer whatever solace she could to remedy to his sorrow.

'What happened, Matt?'

'My fiancée, Victoria, walked out on me.'

'And she told you whilst you were at the vicarage?'

'No, she didn't have the courage to do anything so forthright. She just didn't show up.'

'Show up?'

'At the church. She left me standing at the altar in St Andrew's. Sent her father to deliver the bombshell. Carole and the Rev were awesome. It was as though they'd been through similar situations hundreds of times. I know I was in shock. They put the vicarage at our disposal and my whole family rallied around to smooth over the after-effects, but the worst thing was that I had no idea why Victoria had done it. Not an inkling that anything was wrong.'

'Matt, I'm so sorry…'

Rosie's heart performed a summersault of anguish on Matt's behalf as she pictured him standing next to his best man waiting for his bride to walk down the aisle, but instead seeing her father approach. She couldn't conceive of how devastating that must have been and Matt's experience certainly put what had happened with Harry into perspective. She had loved

Harry, but they hadn't been engaged, nor, now she came to think about it, had they even discussed marriage despite being in the wedding industry. Only now did that strike her as odd, but there would be time later to consider this new realization.

She held Matt's gaze as he fought the returning memories of that painful episode in his life before offering her a rueful smile. Unsurprisingly his response was as pragmatic as she had expected.

'Actually, I've come to terms with what happened, view it as a positive really. We were clearly not right for each other, but I just wish Victoria had had the balls to tell me before everyone had invested their hard-earned cash in their wedding outfits and taken their seats in the pews! My aunt Florence saved up for months to buy her hat, and my cousin used her precious few days' annual leave to come down from Scotland for our wedding. However, I'm pleased to report that she's happy. She's engaged to a Spanish guy called Raphael who has a yacht in the Mediterranean. It was over a year ago, but I still can't face going back to the vicarage.'

'Matt, I'm...'

'Right, enough of the emotional interlude. Want to continue with the shoot? I promise to steer clear of the Ultimate Adventures personalized therapy service from now on!' Matt joked a little unconvincingly. 'It's good to talk, and where better than surrounded by members of the woodland community who won't judge you for your frailties or repeat your words in gossip?'

Rosie took the hint, but something had shifted in their relationship, something intangible that caused a warm, fuzzy feeling at the base of her stomach to glow like an ember of hope, hope that when the current ordeal was over, perhaps there would be something much more pleasurable they could apply their investigation skills to.

'Agreed. Okay, Legolas, brace yourself. I think archery could just be my new favourite pastime. Where's the next target?'

Rosie followed Matt around the archery field course and by the time they had finished she was getting the hang of how to hold the bow and had scored two hits out of the six. Matt had regaled her with several anecdotes about previous groups who had booked the course, one of whom had insisted on having photographs of their board of directors pinned to the targets.

Chapter 14

When they arrived back at Ultimate Adventures' reception area, Matt guided her to one of the leather armchairs and promised her a coffee to thaw her frozen fingers. She tried not to think about the jumble of washing up in the sink she had seen earlier, nor the cleanliness of the mug he offered to her with a smile. She took a sip and sighed. Coffee really did solve a great deal of life's problems.

'So, now that the fun bit of the day is over, we need to apply all our efforts to finding out who could have put aconitine in Suki's throat spray. It has to be someone who knows all about the toxicity of wild flowers and their effects, because if it were me and I wanted to poison someone, my first weapon of choice would be rat poison.'

'Surely you don't think Freddie...'

'No, absolutely not! I believe what he told us in the Drunken Duck about what happened at the lodge. But don't you think it was curious the way Suki lured Freddie there, sobered up, and evicted him almost immediately. If she just wanted to make Felix jealous it was a despicable thing to do.'

'And anyway, Felix wasn't even at the party.'

Rosie bit into one of the chocolate biscuits Matt had put on a plate, holding her hand under her chin to catch the crumbs, then licking them from her palm with the tip of her tongue.

'Little Miss Clean and Tidy strikes again!' Matt smirked before his features settled into a more serious expression. 'Felix was bound to find out about Freddie from one of their friends, though – Nadia probably. She's got envy scrawled across her forehead in capital letters.'

'But why send Freddie away so quickly? Surely she could have let him down gently. Shared a glass of champagne with him as compensation for humiliating him. No wonder he slunk out the back way and decided to hide out here at Ultimate Adventures. My guess is she snagged that bottle of champagne because she was expecting someone. Who though? Do you think it could just have been that Felix called or texted to let her know he was on his way?'

'Possibly.'

'What? You think it could be someone else? Who?'

'Not sure.'

'There's only William, her best friend's boyfriend, or Lucas, her sister's. You're not seriously suggesting she was having an affair with one of them, are you?'

'I'm not suggesting anything.'

'Well, who else is there?' Rosie raked her brain until her eyes widened. 'Not the Rev!'

Matt spluttered into his coffee, sending a shower of droplets into the air.

'Oh my God! Did you just say that? I suggest you stop

right there with your deductions, Rosie, before you give me a heart attack! Anyway, all this is pure speculation.'

But Rosie couldn't get the incident out of her mind. The conundrum continued to spin around her brain on an eternal loop until she thought she would go crazy.

'Who would want to hurt Suki? I don't know her very well, I admit, but she seems lovely. She really looks after her sister, who's definitely a cupcake short of a topping, if you ask me. Heavens, Suki even paid for everyone to stay in the lodges. It's not cheap so she's generous as well. She paid for all the champagne and prosecco for the party *and* she made a decent contribution to the Windmill Café's garden party charities.'

'Her parents were quite wealthy, though,' added Matt, stroking his chin in thought.

'How do you know that?'

'A quick search of the internet threw up all the information. They died in a helicopter crash ten years ago. Their money was put into trust for their two daughters until they reached the age of twenty-five. Suki's twenty-six so she's already got control of her half, and she's one of the trustees for Jess's share which she can use for her sister's maintenance, education and welfare. I bet it was also Suki's money that was paying for their villa rental in Ibiza, but their uncle and aunt are rich, too. Apparently, the cash is from a family business set up by the two Richards brothers – Bill and Ken. Ken Richards has been running things, with his wife Martha as company secretary, since his brother's and sister-in-law's deaths. That information I gleaned from Companies House.'

'Oh my God! Step aside Sherlock Holmes, there's a new kid on the block!'

Rosie saw Matt flash her a brief look of vacillation as he struggled with whether to utter his next sentence. From his expression, she wondered if he was going to talk about his ex-fiancée again, but was shocked when he inhaled a deep breath and revealed something even more personal.

'Actually, you've hit the nail on the head. It was my childhood dream to become a police detective, but unfortunately life had other plans. I used to love solving all kinds of brain-teasers and was an avid watcher of all the TV detective series. When I was eleven, my dad let me help him design the obstacle course at Ultimate Adventures. We argued because I wanted it to be not only a physical challenge, but also a test of the participant's mental agility by using complicated puzzles to unlock each hurdle; it's still one of our most popular activities.'

'So why didn't you join the police force?'

Matt swallowed down the dregs of his coffee and paused, fiddling with the handle of his empty mug, his eyes glazed as his memories scooted back to the reasons for his change of career direction. Their frank conversation during the archery shoot had introduced a carousel of emotions Rosie hadn't been expecting. Coupled with what was going on with Suki, she thought her head would explode from sensation overload. Eventually, Matt banged his mug back to the table, clearly regretting his sudden openness, and forced a wide smile onto his lips.

'Now it looks like there's a real-life whodunnit for us to

crack right here in Willerby! There's no need to worry about the arrival of the environmental health inspectors tomorrow, because between us we'll have the mystery of Suki Richards's poisoning solved before they've had time to fill out their documents in triplicate.'

'Back to the amateur sleuthing, eh?' grinned Rosie, relieved to see the return of Matt's inherent upbeat enthusiasm. 'So, my question is, Detective Inspector Wilson, if someone *did* poison Suki, why? Was it for her money?'

'It usually is. Money or love.'

'Well, I'm going to plump for the love angle.'

'Okay, so what's your theory?' Matt smiled, enjoying her attempt at mystery solving.

'Well, I really don't want to think it's one of Suki's friends – that's just too awful to contemplate. So, could it be someone from Suki's past, someone who's been stalking her for years, following the ups and downs of her music career, convinced that the lyrics of her songs are directed at him and his unswerving love for her? Maybe he'd recently made his affections public and he's been waiting for his chance to punish her for rejecting his advances. She's been living in Ibiza over the summer so he's been biding his time until she came back to the UK and when he found out she'd be in Norfolk opening a summer garden party, he took matters into his own hands and...'

'Are you saying you publicized the Windmill Café's party to the whole country?'

'I, well, I... maybe he *lives* in Norfolk!' Rosie tried not to be offended that her over-inflated theory had been punctured by Matt's injection of common sense and then smiled. 'Okay, who's top of your list of suspects?'

Rosie had been so focused on her conversation with Matt that she hadn't noticed that Mia and Freddie had appeared on the threshold and were listening to their discussion.

'If you want my opinion, I'd start with that William guy,' declared Freddie, his face filled with animation at being able to make his contribution to their speculations. 'I might not be the most perceptive of people, but something's obviously going on between him and Suki. Even if he had nothing to do with the poisoning – even if it turns out it was some sort of an accident – as Suki's manager he should be taste-testing everything, and I mean everything, that she eats or drinks! If he's not guilty of anything else, he's guilty of negligence at the very least!'

'And he did leave the party early to take a shower!' added Mia, plonking herself down on the sofa next to Rosie.

'So, what are we waiting for?' Freddie strode towards the door, eager to seek his revenge, his eyes blazing with indignation. 'Let's nail the scumbag! That guy set me up and I'm not letting him get away with it. I could have been arrested, spent the night in the cells, or worse, I could have been charged with attempted murder!'

'I don't blame you for being angry, Fred, but it's probably best if you stay away from the café for the time being.'

'Why?'

'Let's just say, Felix Dawson is not overjoyed about the fact you went back to Suki's lodge with her.'

'Ah, yes, her elusive boyfriend. Where was he, anyway?'

'That's what I'd like to know too.'

'Actually, if I had to put my money on someone having something to hide, it would *not* have been William,' mused Rosie. 'He's the most straightforward person amongst all of them. And why would he work so hard to get Suki a record deal if he intended to slip a dose of poison in her throat spray so she couldn't perform? It doesn't make any sense. If he loses his star performer, he loses everything. But Matt's right, the perpetrator has to be one of Suki's friends – someone who knew she relied heavily on her throat spray and chose that as their way to deliver the poison. All we have to do is find out who and why.'

'Yeah, that's all!' laughed Freddie.

'Hang on, my phone's ringing.' Matt stood up and extricated his mobile from the pocket of his jeans. 'Hi Carole.' He paused, his eyes resting on Rosie, the sides of his lips twitching as he listened to the vicar's wife.

'Carole...' Another pause.

'Listen, Carole...' She was clearly in full flow.

'Yes, it's true. It seems Suki *was* poisoned, but it was in her...'

'No, Carole...'

'Stop! No one suspects the WI's Victoria sponge cakes... or your egg-and-cress sandwiches with horseradish sauce.' Then Matt laughed. 'It's okay, Carole, I know why you're hesitating – neither was it my mother's home-made sausage rolls!'

Chapter 15

They left a very disgruntled Freddie behind at Ultimate Adventures with promises to meet him later in the Drunken Duck to relay every detail they managed to uncover. Rosie had agreed with Matt that if they were going to take their investigations seriously the first thing they needed to do was dig deeper into Suki's friends' backgrounds. Butterflies were having a disco in her stomach on the drive back to the café as she wondered if the inspectors might have turned up early, but when the car park came into view she saw with relief that the only vehicles there belonged to their guests.

'Hey, is that William?' asked Mia pointing through the windscreen of Matt's SUV.

'Perfect,' said Matt swinging the steering wheel towards the parking space next to William's dark green MG. 'Never look a gift horse in the mouth, as my mum's so fond of saying! Looks like we've got our first interviewee.'

Rosie understood what Matt had in mind. She jumped down from the passenger seat and strolled over to where Suki's business manager was loitering, his forehead creased into parallel lines. She saw him shoot an impatient glance towards the veranda of the lodge he shared with Nadia, the expression on his face making it obvious they'd had a row.

'Hi, William. Are you on your way out somewhere?'

'Not really, just needed to get out for some fresh air. Our lodge has suddenly become a little claustrophobic.'

'Well, it looks like it's about to rain. Fancy joining us for a coffee in the windmill? We've still got some of Suki's scones left from earlier.'

'Great.'

Matt and William settled down on the over-stuffed sofas in the café whilst Rosie helped Mia assemble a tray of coffee. She added a bottle of French brandy she'd been given by Graham as a welcome-to-your-new-home gift when she'd arrived in May. She loathed the taste, but it seemed like this was the perfect time to give it its first outing. From the way the men slung it into their coffee mugs she knew she had been right.

She took a seat on the adjacent sofa, her stomach churning with rampaging nerves. But she couldn't chicken out now, not when the future of the Windmill Café was at stake. She longed to talk to her father, to ask his advice on what she needed to do in order to elicit the right information in such circumstances. How she wished this was simply another one of the murder mystery parties they used to drag her mother and Georgina to at Christmas, where she had fun pitching her mind against his in an effort to be the first to solve the crime and steal the prize.

However, this was real life – yet, weren't the principles the same? They had to narrow down the suspects and one of the ways to do that was by seeking out possible motives, which meant delving into their backgrounds.

'William, would it be okay if Matt and I asked you a few questions? We really want to find out how this dreadful incident could have happened.'

'Do you think I don't? When I get my hands on the person who did this, well, let's just say you wouldn't want to be in the vicinity!'

Rosie watched William lean forward and rest his forearms on his thighs, his back arched to the ceiling. When he raised his head, she noticed the dark smudges beneath his eyes and how untidy his collar-length hair was from the way he dragged his fingers through the waves as he struggled to put his brain into gear to answer her question.

'Ask away! What do you want to know?'

'Well, we thought if we could gather as much information as possible, it might help us to understand how such a deadly poison found its way into Suki's throat spray, who put it there and why. So, can I ask you, whose idea was it to come to Norfolk?'

William knocked back his coffee and refilled his empty mug with neat brandy before levelling his eyes at Rosie and heaving a long, ragged sigh.

'Suki wanted to have one last big get-together with the people she loves before things got manic. She and Jess spent some of their childhood in Norfolk and Felix knew about this place. Suki thought it sounded perfect and insisted on paying for everyone to come for the week. Bill and Angela left her financially secure and she wanted to share it with her family and friends. She's an amazing woman!'

There was now no doubt in Rosie's mind that Freddie had been right – there was definitely more than a business relationship between William and Suki.

'How long have you and Nadia known Suki? You're clearly very close?'

'We all met at university. We took the same music degree course in Sheffield. It was my second degree. I'd already fulfilled my parents' dreams by graduating from Oxford and I thought it was about time to start focussing on my own ambitions. We kept in touch after uni, though. Not only did we have our love of music in common, but I live in Artà, in Majorca, with my parents – they run a tennis academy there – and Suki's uncle and aunt also live there for half the year. Kenneth Richards is Suki and Jess's paternal uncle. He pays the rent on their villa when Suki and Nadia are working in the resorts for the summer. So, whenever they come out, we get together. I can usually manage to pull a few favours and get them a couple of gigs in one of the bars for the summer season in Majorca, but this year they got bookings in Ibiza.'

'So how did you and Nadia get together?' Rosie pressed, starting to feel more confident in her role as examiner-in-chief, keen to know more about the state of their relationship and only a little uncomfortable that it was really none of her business.

'Been together since Christmas. I sort of fell into managing both Nadia's and Suki's music careers, even when they were back in the UK. My first degree is in law and business studies. I handle my parents' tennis academy business, too. My family all adore Suki and Jess – welcomed them both into our lives, especially as their own parents aren't around. Jess even stays with them sometimes in the holidays. She's studying for an English Lit degree – says she wants to be a children's author and illustrator, but my brother, Antonio, thinks she has the potential to make a great tennis player if she'd put a bit more effort in. Or she did until she met Lucas. Pain in the butt, he is. Talks about nothing else except becoming a famous chef and living the "celebrity lifestyle". I know I shouldn't say this, but if you want my opinion, he's only with Jess for her cash.'

Rosie wondered if it was the desire to find the instigator of Suki's suffering or the alcohol that was loosening William's tongue. Should she persuade him to go back to his lodge in case he regretted his honesty the next morning? Would that be the right thing to do? It seemed her initial opinion of William was the right one – he was one of the most straight-forward and candid people she had met. However, before she could say anything, Matt had snatched the enquiry baton from her hands.

'You mean the Richards family trust fund?'

'Yes. Jess isn't due to inherit her share for a few years, but Suki has hers so she spoils Jess. Of course, why shouldn't she? She's her little sister and she lost her parents when she was only eleven. Jess is hopeless when it comes to finances; well, anything that requires a cogent thought process, actually. Suki is really worried about what will happen when Jess turns twenty-five and she inherits her share of the trust fund capital.'

'So what's your theory on what happened?'

William paused, his eyes resting on Matt.

'Well, didn't we all see her drag your *friend* off to her lodge?'

Matt ignored the implication. 'And you didn't see her again until we found her in her lodge in agony?'

'No.'

'Are you sure?'

William stared at Matt for what seemed like an eternity. Then, to Rosie's astonishment, he burst into tears.

'Okay, okay. I went to see her in her lodge. I'm so sorry, the charade at the party was a cover. Suki and I, well, we're in love. She planned on telling Felix as soon as he arrived from Colchester. I was going to break it off with Nadia when we left here so she could go to her parents in Cambridge instead of back with Suki and Jess to Ibiza. The bottle of champagne she snagged on the way to the lodge was for us to celebrate.'

'Well, I don't think Freddie's going to be in a hurry to forgive you when he hears that confession,' muttered Mia. 'You could have saved him a great deal of anguish if you'd spoken up earlier.'

'I'm sorry about what Suki and I put your friend through, I really am. I *will* make sure I apologize to him when I see him. I've been attracted to Suki since I met her at uni, but there was always some guy lurking around so I never made a move. Suki came over to Artà without Jess at the beginning of May and we spent an idyllic two weeks together playing tennis and taking the bikes to the beach. We didn't mean it to happen, but we fell in love. Then she was spotted by a contact of mine from Mountside Records and the recording deal followed. I couldn't dump Nadia right after that and take up with Suki. How would that have looked? I'm not that

cruel, even though the offer of a contract came weeks after
we got together. We wanted to celebrate in secret because
Nadia was crushed.'

'And did you celebrate?'

'Yes, Suki cracked open the Moët and we toasted our future
together, made a few plans. I swear she was the happiest I've
ever seen her when I left the lodge. At last, the world was
smiling on her and she deserves it after everything she's been
through. She's beautiful, a talented performer, a wonderful
friend and a fabulous sister to Jess.' William drew in a steadying breath. 'Do you really think someone wanted to hurt
Suki?'

'I'm not sure. Maybe they just meant to incapacitate her
so she couldn't sing for us on the terrace that night. She did
seem to recover quickly after she had emptied her stomach.'

For the first time since they had bumped into William in
the car park, Rosie saw his features relax and his face morphed
into the attractive and athletic man that Suki had fallen in
love with on the sun-filled tennis courts of Majorca. She
watched him drain the contents of his mug and pushed
himself to his feet a little unsteadily – after all, he had
consumed almost a mugful of Cognac.

'Can I ask you one last question?' asked Rosie. 'What time
did you leave Suki's lodge?'

'I watched Freddie leave and I went straight in. We were
together for about thirty minutes, then I left so she could get
some rest before getting changed for the promised gig and
our dinner afterwards.'

'Did anyone see you leave?'

'I shouldn't think so. We were keeping our relationship secret.'

'Did *you* see anyone, anyone at all, loitering around?'

'No. I went back to my lodge for a quick shower, and then joined Nadia, Jess and Lucas on the terrace. Felix had just arrived and was letting his mouth go. I think he was drunk. The sooner Suki ditches the moron, the better.'

William must have had enough of the interrogation spotlight because he purposefully strode towards the French doors, turning back to the threesome sitting on the sofas, their eyes fixed on his agonized expression. 'Find out who did this, please. For Suki's sake.' And he was gone.

'Well, I think we can strike William from our list of suspects,' said Mia. 'Which leaves us with four people – Felix, Nadia, Jess and Lucas. Who's next on your hit list, Monsieur Poirot? Felix? Can't say I like the guy, and if it's true that he was just about to be dumped...'

'He wouldn't try to poison Suki just because she was going to dump him – that's crazy,' spluttered Matt.

'This whole situation is crazy!'

Rosie stared out of the French doors through which William had disappeared. Twilight was beginning to send fissures of scarlet and mauve through the sky and the starlings had embarked on an evening sonata which gave the deserted terrace a rather sombre feel.

'I'm exhausted. I think we should call it a day,' declared Mia. 'Are you sure I can't talk you into coming to stay with me?'

'Thanks, but I think I'll be fine here. I'll see you tomorrow.'

After thanking Matt for the archery lesson, Rosie turned to encircle Mia in an appreciative hug. Her time in Willerby had taught her that there was no greater magic than the acceptance and support of friends. She couldn't prevent herself from running her eyes over Matt's retreating figure as he made his way back to his SUV in the Windmill Café car park. Every inch of his physique rippled with muscular strength and a surprise fizzle of interest shot through her veins, spreading into her fingertips like pins and needles.

'Matt does ooze a certain rugged charisma, doesn't he?' mused Mia, standing next to Rosie on the terrace to swell the members of the Matt Wilson Appreciation Society.

'Mmm, maybe.'

Rosie waved her friends off and went back inside, careful to lock the door behind her. She cast her eyes around the Windmill Café, a place that should, under happier circumstances, have reverberated with the clatter and chatter of culinary activity and animated conversation. Silence wrapped its insidious fingers around the room in a way that was somehow hypnotic and served to calm her anxieties. She cleared away their coffee mugs, washed them slowly in soapy water and put them back in their allocated places, then sprayed the benches with disinfectant.

She climbed the stairs to her circular studio, her bones weighed down with a heavy lethargy, and slumped onto the sofa. She couldn't stop her brain from spinning with a merry-go-round of emotions and a migraine threatened, so she grabbed one of her favourite cookery books – The Great British Baking Bazaar – and began leafing through the glossy pages.

Both her parents had adored books, but their favoured genres occupied opposite ends of the reading spectrum. Rosie remembered the first time she was allowed to choose her own book from the local library in the Hampshire village where she grew up, and her mother had told her the story that every one of the precious tomes contained a tiny fragment of the author's heart so Rosie had to treat them with respect and reverence, irrespective of her personal preference as to subject matter.

In the dark days after her father's death, her mother's love of Mills & Boon was one of the few things that had pulled her through. Rosie too had relied on the stories she read to transport her to another place, far away from the clutches of reality, but recently, with the little peppermint-and-white windmill in her life and Mia by her side, she had let her reading habit slip.

She decided to curl up in bed with one of her father's old gardening books that accompanied her everywhere. Yet, despite her determination to sink into a good book, Rosie slipped into the oblivion of sleep within seconds of her head hitting her silk pillowcase.

Chapter 16

Rosie awoke feeling refreshed and eager to attack the day ahead. As the early morning sun splashed its rays through the windows causing dust eddies to bounce across the room on beams of light, she felt her creative juices flowing. For once, it was not the usual tingle in her fingers to grab the nearest dishcloth and disinfectant spray, but an unscratchable urge to delve her hands into a bowl of flour. Food preparation – be it baking, roasting, poaching, scrambling or sautéing – had become her solace in the place of flower arranging and she loved every single stage of it, not just the cleaning up.

For some reason, her thoughts lingered briefly on Harry. Of course, things hadn't always been so hostile between them. The initial blossoming of her love for Harry, and being allowed to work alongside him in the flower shop, had helped to chase away her past anxieties and she found she was able to rekindle her passion for plant-based activities once again. Over time, she had got used to the daily contact with dirty water, soil and mould and slowly but surely, she managed to suppress the hygiene beasts too. Okay, she knew they were lurking in the darkest, grimmest corners of her mind, but she had been determined not to feed them with tasty morsels of her emotional wellbeing. She had been happy, relaxed and content with her life, which was why discovering Harry with Heidi had been such a shock.

Georgina had reported visiting the little flower shop when she had been shopping for her birthday present in the capital in July, but there had been no sign of the woman who had replaced her in Harry's affections. Maybe she could have come to terms with Harry's infidelity sooner if he'd chosen a different person to share his bed with. The scandal had just been too much to bear at the time. However, if Heidi hadn't decided to slot her size eights into Rosie's bejewelled sandals, she knew she would never have relocated to Norfolk, which meant she would never have explored her flair for culinary enterprise, nor met Mia, Matt and Freddie.

Rosie's fear of relationships had not completely evaporated, but her belief that she had lost her identity, her place in the world and everything she held dear, had diffused. She now possessed the burgeoning conviction that she *would* survive, and not only that, but that she could enjoy whatever the director of her destiny had mapped out for her. Instead of standing back and letting life happen around her, Mia had inspired her to take control, to move forward, to seek fulfilment in a different version of her dreams with the same passion, hope and expectation she'd had for her flower business until Harry had burst her bubble.

Over the last four months, her enthusiasm for creating new and exotic recipes, and to try them out on the customers of the little Windmill Café, had blasted forth with frequent regularity and she loved it. With the calm encouragement of Mia, and Georgina, she had been able to turn the page of her autobiography and start to write a new story for her future. She suddenly experienced an intense craving to speak to her sister, to hear her sensible words of advice.

'Hi, Georgie. How're things?'

'Fabulous. I've just been offered a part in a historical drama that's being filmed down here in Hampshire next month. It's only a small role but it should be fun and I'll get to meet Darcie Fowler who's playing the lead! How's that cute little café of yours? Any hunky guys on the horizon? Oh, how did the garden party go at the weekend? At least you had good weather for it!'

Rosie waited for her sister to draw breath. She had always been the more gossipy child as they grew up. Instead of the turmoil of their teenage years causing Georgina to retreat into her shell, Rosie thought it had made her fearless, unafraid of speaking out, of trying something new or putting herself in difficult situations. After all, as her sister repeatedly said, what was the worst that could happen? Georgina's self-confidence had stood her in good stead as she made her way through drama school and onto the stage at the local theatre, and then into small TV roles. Rosie was certain that her sister's star was in the ascendant and that it was only a matter of time before she got a lead actress role in a Hollywood blockbuster.

'Well, if you count poisoning your guests as a successful outcome, then the garden party went swimmingly.'

'What are you talking about?'

Rosie immediately regretted telling Georgina about the disastrous ending to what had been such a wonderful day. She decided to give her the sanitized version of events for fear of having her indignant sister rush to her side and stand guard against unwarranted accusations.

'Oh, it was nothing really. Just one of the guests had a stomach upset and her boyfriend thought it was food poisoning and threatened to call in the food inspectors.'

'Were any of the other guests affected?'

'No, no one else.'

'And you're okay?'

'I'm fine. Don't worry.'

'Didn't her boyfriend realize that there is no way any malicious germ could survive after an encounter with Rosie Barnes and her faithful antibacterial spray?' giggled Georgina.

'Clearly not.'

Rosie prayed that her sister wouldn't dwell on the issue as she had never been good at keeping the truth from her. She cast around in her tangled thoughts for a change of subject but Georgina beat her to it.

'So, tell me more about the summer garden party. Have you emailed photographs to Graham like I suggested? Has he agreed to your suggestion to do an autumnal-themed party yet? What did the guests think of the raspberry and white chocolate cupcakes?'

Rosie spent the next ten minutes playing up the positives of the Windmill Café's first summer party to her sister, almost convincing herself that it had been a total success. She asked for details of the historical drama she was rehearsing for and about the progress of the rock musical her husband Jack was working on. Her mood started to lift as it always did when she and Georgina spent time gossiping, until the inevitable question was asked.

'And are you really expecting me to believe that there was not one hot-blooded male at the party? Or in the whole of Willerby for that matter?'

'Well, I...'

'Oooh, there is! Spill the details, Rose. Come on, please, Jack is about as romantic as a wet fish at the moment. It's this damn musical he's got himself involved in, it's eating up every spare bit of his time and more. Actually, I was thinking of coming up to Norfolk and bunking up with you in that cute little windmill of yours for a few days until opening night or I think I might just go crazy.'

Panic spread across Rosie's chest. The last thing she wanted was for Georgina to discover what was going on and put on her metaphorical deerstalker. She had to deflect her suggestion without upsetting her or raising her suspicions about the café, or indeed organizing her wedding to the first unattached guy she set her eyes on – suitable or otherwise.

'Matt and I are just friends...'

'Does he work at the café?'

'No. He owns an outward-bound centre in the village...'

'Ah, so he's a real-life hunk? He must be if he spends his days scrambling over obstacle courses, riding quad bikes and flying along zip wires! Has he invited you to go yomping with him yet? Or skinny dipping?'

'No, Georgie, he has not. As I said, we're just friends.'

'Friends can turn into lovers, you know, Rosie.'

Rosie managed to deflect her sister's cross-examination to the subject of their mother and her recent penchant for synchronized swimming and they ended the conversation with promises to speak again at the weekend. After they had said their goodbyes, she craved a dose of friendly company, unable to admit to herself that what she really wanted to do was escape the arrival of one of the holiday site guests. She decided to make her second trip in two days to Ultimate Adventures, a place where she knew she would receive a warm welcome.

When she arrived at the outward-bounds centre, the car park was already full of gleaming 4X4's and mud-splattered vans belonging to the people crowding the wooden reception area eager to make a start on that day's schedule of activities. She grabbed a seat on one of the sofas and waited for Freddie to process everyone and send them in the right direction.

'Why don't you come through to the kitchen, Rosie, and I'll make you a brew?' said Freddie, dropping his Ultimate Adventures fleece on the kitchen table and adding to the mountain of chaos already there. She could feel the familiar craving for order rushing through her veins, moving ever upwards until, with huge effort, she forced it from her mind.

'I don't think you've ever made me a cup of tea before! I'm looking forward to this.'

'Don't worry, I'll taste it first and you can wait to see if I keel over and die before you risk taking a sip. I won't be offended. And I don't know about you, but I'm starving – want to take your life in your hands and share an omelette with me, too?'

'You make the tea, Freddie and I'll rustle up the omelettes,' Rosie laughed.

Once again, the task of feeding others came to her rescue. She threw herself into making the fluffiest omelettes possible, whisking the eggs until her hands ached, hunching over the stove and the heavy cast iron frying pan, her eyes smarting from the fragrant steam. The aroma of fresh, herb-filled omelettes served to encourage Matt out of his office. She rummaged in the fridge and tossed together a salad; a combination of lettuce, tomatoes and carrot strips fashioned into broad ribbons, with a 'secret recipe' vinaigrette and they all dug in.

'You make a mean omelette, you know, Rosie. But this salad is... well, different.'

Rosie giggled when she saw Freddie sniff, and then inspect, the ingredients of the salad before raising a forkful into his mouth. What was he expecting to see? Curled purple petals nestling between the rocket and the radicchio? But still, she noticed he waited until Matt had taken a mouthful before devouring his.

Watching them relish every mouthful gave Rosie pause for thought. Maybe she should think more positively about the imminent arrival of the inspectors that day, view the recent upsetting turn of events as part of the patchwork of living life to the full, an event stitched into the rhythm of her life which added to what she would become. She knew for sure that any philosophical acceptance of the possibility she could have no job or home by the weekend was not only down to her affinity with food preparation, but to the man who sat opposite her scraping his plate of the last morsel.

'It's a particularly nasty thing to do though, don't you think?' mused Matt. 'Lacing Suki's throat spray with poison. It's as though someone wanted her to really suffer.'

'But why? She's lovely. She's kind to her sister – even though Jess is a bit flighty. We know William adores her. And she's paid for a week's break in luxury lodges with outdoor spas just because she wanted everyone to have fun. She's generous, popular, well-liked, excited about her future and on the brink of something special. Can it really be one of her friends who did this to her and not an unbalanced fan or spurned admirer who followed Suki here?'

'I'm sure of it, and that person clearly used the spray because they wanted her next live performance to be affected – which leads me to believe it was someone who was envious of her success. What they didn't foresee was that Suki would offer to sing whilst on holiday in Norfolk.'

'What do you mean? Oh!' Freddie picked up on Matt's train of thought. 'Yes! Suki has been offered the recording contract – jealousy. And what if Nadia knew about William and Suki's affair but was biding her time, planning her revenge?'

'It's a theory.'

'And poison. It's not like a blow to the head, is it? In fact, the person didn't even have to be around when Suki took it,' added Rosie.

'Mmm, interesting point, Miss Jessica Fletcher, I think you may be onto something.'

The tinkle of a brass bell reverberated through to the kitchen and interrupted their deductions.

'I'll go,' said Matt, leaping from his chair and striding from the room.

Rosie couldn't stop her eyes from roaming over Matt's strong physique, those broad shoulders, those taut buttocks, and the memory of his firm hands as he'd guided her own on the bow. She could still feel the warmth of his body moulded perfectly next to hers and smell the faint whiff of his aftershave on her jacket.

'Freddie? Can you come out here, please?'

Freddie shoved a whole chocolate biscuit into his mouth and shrugged his shoulders at Rosie. When the kitchen door swung open, Rosie saw who Matt was talking to and her stomach gave a sharp nip of surprise.

'I needed to get away from everyone, so I thought I'd come over here,' explained Nadia. 'Please tell me there's something I can join in with to get rid of all this pent-up energy. If I don't do something soon I think I might explode!'

'Come on, I'll take you over to the climbing wall,' said Matt. 'Freddie, can you hold the fort here, please?'

'Sure.'

'Actually, Rosie had the same idea this morning. Would you mind if she joins us?'

'I don't mind at all.'

When Rosie appeared at the kitchen door, Nadia flicked the sides of her auburn bob behind her ears and attempted a smile. Rosie could see how agitated she was, her hands constantly restless, her eyes jumping from one thing to another and a spasm of sympathy shot into her chest, coupled with a generous helping of apprehension if Matt was expecting her to join Nadia on the climbing wall. She had never been top of the leader board when it came to heights, or ropes, or anything remotely connected with climbing for that matter; Georgina had been the tomboy of the family.

'Here, take these.'

Matt handed each of them an Ultimate Adventures fleece and they followed him to the store room to collect the safety equipment before tramping through to a small clearing at the rear of the office where the climbing wall was situated. Rosie tipped her chin upwards to look at the top and it was so high she almost fell over backwards.

'Looks daunting, doesn't it?' said Nadia, vocalizing Rosie precise thoughts.

'Terrifying!'

'Do you think it's too late for us to back out?'

'Erm...'

Rosie glanced at Matt who was emptying a huge rucksack of gear. 'Sorry, girls, forgotten your elbow guards. Be back in a minute.'

Matt gave Rosie a meaningful stare and an imperceptible nod in Nadia's direction. It was a couple of seconds before she realized what he meant. She tried to shake her head at him but he had already turned his back and sprinted off back to the storeroom. However, if they were to have any chance of finding out who spiked Suki's throat spray and why, she had to grasp the opportunity to ask questions of their suspects whenever it presented itself. She had no idea how to broach the subject of Suki's chance to shoot for stardom, other than to launch straight in.

'So, how do you feel about Suki's record deal?'

Nadia stared at her for a moment and Rosie thought she was going to tell her to mind her own business, but instead her shoulders slumped. She indicated a wooden bench fashioned from what looked like a railway sleeper and started to fiddle with the silver chains at her neck, her eyes fixed on an indeterminate point in the canopy of trees above their heads.

'Suki's my best friend and I'm happy for her. She's worked so hard for her big break – we both did. The music business is a tough industry to make any progress in. If you'd seen some of the places we were booked to perform in you'd appreciate how much a recording deal means to Suki. Sure, I would be lying if I said I didn't wish it had been me, who wouldn't? But I'm not jealous, I'm really not. If I'm brutally honest, she's a much better vocalist than I am. And even if I was jealous, I would never have sabotaged her chances by poisoning her! The contract doesn't transfer to me in the event of her sudden unavailability or anything like that!'

Nadia's face flushed with indignation as she re-tucked her copper-streaked bob behind her ears. Her outfit that day was a lemon, scoop-necked T-shirt embroidered with sunflowers and tight black designer jeans. Rosie knew that Nadia relished displaying her impressive cleavage and had shaped her wardrobe to reflect that – but in the middle of a deserted patch of woodland, she looked out-of-place and out-of-sorts and Rosie felt sorry for her.

'Okay, ready to go now,' announced Matt, handing out the elbow guards.

'You know, I think I might have been a little hasty when I said I wanted to do something to take my mind of things.'

'Nothing worthwhile is ever easy,' said Matt, his dark blond hair standing up in tufts, looking like he'd just left his surfboard behind in the storeroom.

'That's exactly what Suki says before we go on stage. We both suffer from nerves before a gig; Suki more often than me, to be honest. She's always coming out with crazy mantras, and she sticks rigorously to her little pre-show rituals – if she can't find her throat spray, all hell breaks loose. Performers often have little routines before they go on stage – you know the sort of thing – if she has three sprays before a concert it'll go well; if she forgets, or she's run out, or only sprayed twice, it will be a complete disaster and we'll never get a repeat booking. Actually, looking at this climbing wall I could do with a couple of squirts of the magic stuff myself!'

'Mm, me too,' murmured Rosie.

Suddenly Nadia's eyes narrowed at Matt and Rosie. 'I know what people are thinking – that I was so jealous of Suki's record deal that I put something in her spray so she couldn't sing for everyone on Sunday night. That's what you think too, isn't it?'

'Well, you did go to Suki's lodge to change into one of her dresses, so you did have access to...' began Matt.

'We *all* went to Suki's lodge before the party – except for that idiot of a boyfriend of hers. Trust him to be in the clear! If I had to pick a person responsible for this it would be Felix!'

Nadia ripped off her helmet and knee guards and flung them to the ground, ready to take flight until Matt asked softly 'I take it you know William and Suki are having an affair?' and her indignant demeanour deflated as if a needle had been stabbed in a balloon. She crumpled back down onto the bench, twisting one of the silver chains at her throat. A succession of emotions floated across her expression – shock, outrage, acquiescence.

'Yes, I knew,' she whispered, tears trickling down her cheeks.

'And had you spoken to either of them about your suspicions?' asked Rosie, taking a seat beside Nadia. She reached for her hand and was unsurprised to find her fingers were trembling and freezing cold.

'No. To be honest, I was hoping it would fizzle out, but if anything, they seemed to grow closer. I knew William was going to dump me. Actually, I was surprised he didn't do it before we came up to Norfolk.'

'How did you feel about your best friend and your boyfriend being in a relationship?'

'Matt!'

Rosie recognized the hurt in Nadia's eyes and her heart squeezed with empathy. After what had happened with Harry and Heidi she understood exactly how Nadia felt. Taking a few moments to shove her emotions back into their box,

Nadia's habitual spark emerged from the shadows of her pain and she met Matt's eyes with a challenge.

'How do you think I felt? Angry, worthless, sad. I loved him. I still do. But I did *not* try to poison my best friend! If you want to know who did, maybe you should look at the other person scorned! I'm not staying here any longer to be accused of something I had nothing to do with!' Nadia stalked from the clearing, every muscle in her body clenched in anger.

'Matt, why did you have to bring up the affair?'

'Rosie, someone poisoned Suki, and that same person couldn't have cared less about the effect their actions would have on the Windmill Café's future, or yours! And before you say anything else, think about it. Nadia not only had the opportunity to tamper with Suki's throat spray when she changed her outfit, but also a reason for wanting her to suffer discomfort and either cancel her performance or sing badly. There's not only the motive of professional jealousy, which, I might add, was instigated by William, but Suki has also stolen her boyfriend who she's just confessed she still loves.'

Rosie watched Matt stride off towards his office to catch up with Nadia. Would she have spiked Heidi's drink if she had been presented with the opportunity? Of course not, it was Harry she held responsible for the termination of their relationship, not Heidi. Matt was way off course. She had seen the genuine affection in Nadia's eyes when she spoke of her best friend and her flourishing music career and she knew Nadia was another suspect they could strike from the list. They were running out of options and if they didn't find out the truth soon, Rosie suspected the finger of accusation may very well swing back in her direction when Felix discovered her background in floristry.

However, before she could dwell on that scenario, her mobile sprang into life and she knew she had much more pressing matters to deal with. The environmental health inspectors had arrived at the Windmill Café.

Chapter 17

'Thanks for coming with me, Matt. I owe you.'

Anxiety gnawed at her abdomen as they headed back to the café. She had known the inspectors would be arriving at some point that day but it didn't make the fact any easier to accept. When they pulled into the car park at the Windmill Café, her heart lurched as she saw not only Dr Bairstow's Range Rover, but a shiny black 4X4 with blacked-out windows in one of the other spaces. Rosie knew she was being ridiculous, but she had never seen a more ominous vehicle.

'Graham should have made the effort to be back in the UK by now. He could have caught a flight as soon as you called him. It's really not fair to leave you to deal with this on your own! It would be a tragedy if Willerby lost its landmark café and anyone who has ever enjoyed a meal from its kitchen will have been left in no doubt how pristine the place is. You have nothing to worry about, Rosie. We know the cause of Suki's illness was someone spiking her throat spray which was probably carried out before your guests even arrived in Norfolk. All you have to do is meet the inspectors, answer every question they ask, and they'll move on to the next business more deserving of their time and expertise.'

'Thanks, Matt.'

A surge of confidence washed over Rosie. With Matt at her side she felt like she could conquer anything – look how she'd handled her very first attempt at field archery under his careful instruction – although there was a lot more at stake this time. She jumped down from the passenger seat of his SUV and strode across to the café with purpose, keys in her hand.

The day was well into its third act, the sky strewn with bruised clouds threatening a repeat of the earlier rain that had left a slick coating of moisture on the lawns and puddles dotted across the terrace. Rosie pushed back the French doors to let as much light and air into the kitchen as possible.

She took comfort in the fact that whilst she wasn't responsible for the cleaning of the lodges – Graham employed a local business to do that – she had personally checked each lodge before Suki's party had arrived and they were all spotless. Matt was right, she should have more self-belief.

'Okay, I've just been over to Suki and Felix's lodge. Dr Bairstow is there with the two environmental health inspectors,' said Matt, arriving in the café's kitchen and snatching up a slice of cherry flapjack. 'I've told them we'll be waiting for them in the café. I hope they've brought their gas masks because this place stinks of bleach!'

Apprehension swirled around Rosie's body whipping her breath from her lungs. She needed something to do with her hands but there was nothing left for her to clean. She gave

Matt a weak smile, grateful for his support and not wanting to give him the impression that she was anything less than confident in the outcome of the investigation. Sadly, she would never be worthy of an Oscar in the Best Actress category and she knew her fake bravado hadn't fooled him.

'Rosie, I know how stressful this is for you, but you have a lot of friends here who...'

'Are you open? I could murder a cup of tea!'

Dr Bairstow's ruggedly handsome face appeared at the French doors, the bump in his nose testament to his enduring hobby. His shoulders were so broad and muscular, Rosie was surprised his presence didn't block out all the natural light. Her spirits edged up a notch when she saw he was smiling as he rubbed his palm over his bristly beard.

'No problem, take a seat. Dr Bairstow...'

'Philip, please. Suki's still giving her statement to the environmental health guys but it seems she has no idea how the substance could have got into her spray. She makes it herself from a recipe she got off the internet which of course does not include aconitine! We've tested each of the ingredients separately and there's no trace of poison in any of them, including the honey you gave Suki from the kitchen, Rosie. By process of deduction, we now know that the poison was in the bottle itself before she filled it.'

'Does that mean the Windmill Café is in the clear?' asked Rosie, so overwhelmed with relief that she struggled to prevent tears from forming along her lashes.

'Yes, but the inspectors will still want to take a look around before they leave, just as a formality, then I've advised Suki to call the police. Understandably, she is struggling to come to terms with the confirmation that someone intended to cause her harm, someone who knew about and had access to her throat spray.'

'Thanks for coming to tell us,' said Matt, holding out his palm as Rosie put down a pot of Earl Grey and a slice of flapjack in front of Dr Bairstow.

'Ah, Rosie, you're a lifesaver. Would you believe that this is the first food to pass my lips since yesterday lunchtime? My partner is on holiday with his family in Provence and I've been on call for the last week without a break. Mmm, this flapjack is delicious, could I take a couple of pieces with me?'

'Of course, and they're on the house.'

'Do you think you'll reopen the café this afternoon?'

'No,' said Matt before Rosie could even decide what she intended to do. 'I think Rosie and Mia deserve a day off to recharge their batteries. And a trip to the beach is calling our names.'

'Well, have fun, and thanks again for the flapjack, Rosie.'

'It's me who should be thanking you, Doctor... erm, Philip.'

'No thanks necessary. All in a day's work. Catch you later.'

Matt and Rosie waved the doctor off just as Felix arrived on the terrace.

'Ah, Rosie, I was wondering if you could rustle me up a round of your delicious cheese and cucumber sandwiches?' he asked, flashing his incongruously white teeth, his perfectly shaped eyebrows raised in question.

'Actually, the café is closed,' snapped Matt, in case Rosie was thinking of wavering. 'And I would have thought the first thing you should be saying to Rosie, and Mia when you see her, is how sorry you are for throwing around unsubstantiated accusations that could have forced the Windmill Café to close for good, not to mention the fact that Rosie would have lost her home.'

'Of course, I'm filled with remorse,' Felix replied, not looking at all contrite despite supposedly being an accomplished actor.

Rosie took a couple of moments to consider the man lounging against the countertop in her kitchen. Felix Dawson was handsome, there was no denying it; over six feet tall with well-honed muscles, light blond hair that had been enhanced by well-placed highlights, and of course that toothpaste-ad smile. Yes, he was attractive in a plastic kind of a way, but boy did he know it. His pale lilac shirt had been immaculately pressed, not a crease dared to invade its crispness, and his tan was clearly genuine having spent most of the summer at Suki's villa in Ibiza. He gave the impression of someone totally relaxed in his own skin, arrogant even.

She met his eyes and was shocked to experience a frisson of desire curl through her veins. His irises were such a perfect shade of turquoise, they reminded her of the Mediterranean Sea when the midday sun sparkled on the surface of the waves. Clean-shaven, his well-chiselled jawline could have been sculpted by a maestro of design. He exuded a faint hint of woody cologne which invaded her nostrils and added to the pull of attraction, and he had even managed to erase his native Mancunian accent to speak in the rounded tones of a BBC news reporter. But it was his smile that brought Rosie back down to earth. She wouldn't want to be standing next to him in ultraviolet light. She would need to wear her sunglasses or run the risk being blinded.

'Sorry, Felix. Matt and I were just on our way out...'

'But I suppose if it's just a sandwich you're after then we can delay for an hour or so.'

Rosie did a double-take. What was Matt talking about? Hadn't he just informed Felix in no uncertain terms that there would be no food cooked at the Windmill Café that day. She opened her mouth to protest, but saw Matt give her an almost imperceptible wink and took the hint. Clearly he hadn't given up on earning his detective badge just yet.

'One cheese and cucumber sandwich coming up. Do you want a coffee?'

'Please and a slice of that flapjack, if you don't mind.'

As Rosie made her way to the kitchen to put on her apron, she strained her ears to listen in to the conversation as Matt made the perfect opening gambit.

'So, Felix, I hear you're an actor?'

'I am. Actually, I've just finished filming a role as a playboy aristocrat in the next series of a costume drama, Fountain's Abbey. Have you seen it?'

'No, I'm afraid not.'

'It's set in the Scottish Highlands. I play...'

'And how long have you and Suki been together?'

'Oh, yes, well, let me see. I met Suki, William and Nadia at Sheffield University about five years ago, but Suki and I didn't get together as a couple until January this year. We bumped into each other at a New Year's Eve wrap party for a TV detective series I'd been in and we've been together ever since.'

'Do you live together?'

Rosie put the sandwich down in front of Felix, turning her head slightly so she could raise her eyebrows at Matt without Felix noticing. She was surprised, and a little concerned, that Felix didn't seem in the slightest bit reticent about answering Matt's somewhat intrusive questions. But then, he was clearly one of those people who relished every opportunity to talk about themselves and their careers.

'I moved into Suki's flat in Kensington in March. She went out to Majorca at the beginning of May to stay with William's parents and to sort out a villa to rent in Ibiza for the summer. I followed a couple of weeks later – with Jess in tow. You've seen what she's like, probably would have ended up in a harem in Bahrain if I hadn't been with her. William and Nadia also rented a place in San Antonio, but it wasn't a patch on Suki's – much to Nadia's disgust. She was always round at our place, lazing by the pool, eating our food, drinking our booze. Should have seen her face when William announced he'd got Suki a recording contract. I was expecting a catfight.'

'How did *you* feel when Suki was offered the recording deal?' asked Rosie, getting drawn into the story as more details of Suki's life emerged.

'Well, we had a fabulous celebration at Suki's favourite restaurant in Santa Eulalia. We drank so much champagne that night I don't remember much about it to be honest. Of course, I was ecstatic that she'd finally achieved her dream. So ecstatic, in fact, I proposed.'

'You proposed!' gasped Rosie, sloshing the coffee she had been in the process of pouring into Matt's cup onto the table, and then rushing back to the kitchen for a cloth.

'Yes. I loved her. She loved me. Why not?'

'But?'

Rosie cast a swift glance in Matt's direction, but his face remained a mask of concentration as he stared straight back at Felix. For the first time, she saw Felix's polished exterior slip. His forehead wrinkled, his eyes narrowed and his incongruous movie-star teeth were subjected to an onslaught of grinding.

'She turned me down. It was that moron, William Morgan! He advised her not to jeopardize her one shot at fame and fortune by getting engaged on the spur of the moment. He told her to take her time to think it through, to maybe postpone any engagement until the new album was in the bag. But then there would be the promotion, the live tours...' Felix's upper lip curled and his stare held an intensity bordering on hatred.

'How did you manage your acting career while you and Suki were in Ibiza?' asked Rosie.

'Well, the summer months are often a quiet time in my profession. I've had a couple of supporting actor roles, but it's a difficult business to make a decent living out of, especially when you don't have a trust fund or Mummy and Daddy's tennis academy to fall back on. Some of us have to work our butts off just to stay afloat.'

'So, you were envious of Suki's success when your own career hit a lull, and of her friendship with William,' concluded Matt.

'I wasn't envious! I was delighted for her. I asked her to marry me, for God's sake!'

'Could that be because you didn't want to lose her once she got sucked into the maelstrom of a singing career? Or were you afraid she would gallop off into the sunset leaving you behind in her slipstream?'

'Of course not. What are you suggesting? Hey, what is this? Some sort of an interrogation?' The scorch of Felix's glare could ignite paper as he scraped back his chair, intending to storm out of the café.

However, Matt wasn't going to give up. 'Look, Felix, Dr Bairstow has told us that the police are getting involved. This is serious – for all we know someone could have been trying to *kill* Suki! Rosie and I simply want to try to find out whatever we can to help solve the mystery before that happens. It's in everyone's interests, don't you think? You're Suki's boyfriend – you'll be on their list of suspects, probably at the top!'

Felix was gobsmacked at what Matt had just said. Clearly that possibility had not even occurred to him. Rosie saw alarm reflected in his gaze and it was obvious that Matt had pierced his carefully-crafted armour of arrogance. She grabbed the tray of flapjacks, slid it onto the table in front of Felix and plonked herself down at the table, hoping to calm the situation with an injection of sugar.

'Was it your idea to book the lodges here in Willerby?' Rosie asked after a few moments.

'Yes. What's that got to do with anything?' Felix's face had taken on a sullen, almost petulant look and the tremble of his hands belied a nicotine addict denied his regular fix.

'Actually, if you want to know, I thought coming here would be the perfect opportunity to change Suki's mind about the engagement – away from all the excitement of the music scene and the distractions of San Antonio.'

'But you spent most of the weekend on a pub crawl with your friends in Colchester, didn't you? That's not the behaviour of a man who wants to romance his girlfriend into accepting a marriage proposal.'

'Can't a guy have a night off? Look, I know where you're going with this, and I don't blame you. I shouldn't have jumped to conclusions about the food at the garden party. I'm sorry, okay? And if you think I had anything to do with spiking Suki's spray, then you're way off base. I adore Suki, and so does my family, especially my sister. Josie's hoping to become the sister-in-law of a famous pop star – you know, free concert tickets, backstage passes, autographs, boasting rights.'

'So what's your theory on the throat spray?'

'It must have been some sort of accident. Using the spray is like an obsession for Suki. It was like, if she didn't have her throat spray with her, plus a couple of back-ups in her bag, she just couldn't go on stage. Ridiculous, but it usually worked to calm her nerves. I have no idea how that weird poison got into the bottle. She sterilizes them religiously.'

'Did Suki ever use anything else before a performance?' asked Rosie.

'Never. And to be honest she wasn't much of a drinker either. When I heard about her downing a couple of bottles of champagne and taking a bottle of Moët off to the lodge

174

with that guy, I couldn't believe it, but now I've had a chance to think things through I understand why Suki did that.'

'Really?'

'I promised to come up to Norfolk for the garden party as soon as I was sober enough to drive. I was late. I missed the party. She was angry. She wanted to teach me a lesson so she made a show of copping off with some random stranger. Nothing happened and she ditched him as soon as they were out of sight of that gossipmonger, Nadia. Suki and I are destined to be together. If only that idiot William hadn't stuck his size nines in, we'd be engaged now. I wouldn't have had to persuade her to come to this boring backwater and we'd still be relaxing on our sun-loungers soaking up the Spanish rays.'

'So if someone told you that Suki was having an affair you wouldn't believe them?'

Felix's eyes widened and locked onto Matt's gaze. Two red spots appeared on his cheeks and his mouth gaped as he held his coffee mug at his lips.

'Absolutely not!'

This time Felix couldn't engage his acting skills to disguise his emotions. His face drained of all colour leaving a hard, leathery expression that Rosie found discomforting. Beads of perspiration collected on his upper lip and at his temples. As he raised his fingertips to wipe away the moisture, his hand shook and barely restrained anger exuded from every pore of his body.

To Rosie's intense relief, Matt accepted that he had gone too far with his questions. If he had been a character in was one of her father's favourite American detective novels, this was the part where the investigator got beaten up for his troubles and she certainly didn't want to be the one to have to separate the two of them.

'Great, thanks Felix. It's been good chatting to you. We'll let you get back to your friends now.'

Felix glared at Matt, his fists curled into balls, but he stood up from the table, tossed down a twenty-pound note, and strode from the café without another word.

'I thought he was going to hit you. Why did you have to ask him that?'

'Like Nadia, Felix knows William and Suki are having an affair. I'd put money on it, which gives him a motive for putting something in her spray, don't you think?'

'If you want my honest opinion, I don't think Felix is the culprit. He's got too much to lose, not just Suki, but he's genuinely focussed on his own acting career and I don't think he would jeopardize that for anything. Matt, you're not Poirot. Now that the Windmill Café is off the hook and the police are getting involved, I think you should leave the sleuthing up to the authorities. Anyway, didn't you promise me a trip to the beach?'

Chapter 18

Matt parked his SUV in the car park overlooking the beach. The day still held some of its warmth and a mild summer breeze toyed with the grasses on the dunes. A wide crescent of golden sand swept northwards, but it was the expanse of sparkling blue sea that whipped Rosie's breath away. Most families had returned home for the day, leaving only the water sports enthusiasts and the occasional dog walker to claim the sands as their own. Having lived in London for two years, the scene spread out before her looked like paradise.

'You are so lucky to have spent your childhood here, Matt,' sighed Rosie, drinking it all in.

'I know. We used to come down to the beach every day after school. My brother Tom and I even had a small boat until the idiot managed to sink it during some charade when he was celebrating the end of his exams! Come on!' Matt grabbed her hand and together they jogged towards the sea, kicking up sand in their wake.

'Hang on!'

Rosie paused in her sprint to remove her shoes, laughing as her hair flew into the air like a wild Medusa on steroids before slapping her in the face. With the smell of the sea in her nostrils and the sand between her toes, she felt as if all her woes had melted into oblivion and the only thing that mattered was enjoying the moment. A surge of contentment invaded her body and the person she had to thank for that was standing right by her side with a mischievous glint in his eyes. Her heart performed a swift flip-flop and she parted her lips to say something, to thank him for his friendship, but she was reluctant to break the spell that Matt seemed to have cast over them on the idyllic Norfolk beach. Then she saw his dimples deepen, his dark blue eyes widen and she knew immediately what he had in mind.

'No!'

'Yes!'

Matt grasped her hand firmly in his and dragged her towards the waves.

'Matt!'

'Having fun?'

Despite her reluctance to be splashed with freezing cold water, she had to admit that she couldn't remember the last time she'd had so much fun. Matt seemed to possess a talent for squeezing every ounce of enjoyment out of any occasion.

'Argh!'

Rosie entered the sea at full pelt and droplets of cold water splashed up her naked legs and onto her forearms. She let go of Matt's hand and reached down into the waves, scooped up a handful of water and tossed it in Matt's direction, scoring a direct hit. The shock on his face at her antics made her giggle.

'Okay, Miss Barnes, if that's how you want to play it, you'd better watch out!'

Within seconds she too was soaked. She tried to run away from the onslaught of freezing water, but she was no match for Matt who had probably played more water games than she had baked cupcakes. Her T-shirt clung to her chest and her hair was a straggly mess, yet she didn't care. Sartorial elegance didn't matter one iota to Matt – another reason to love him!

What? Rosie paused in her escape towards the beach. What had she just said to herself?

The brief hesitation cost her dearly because before she knew what was happening, Matt lunged at her from behind and she tumbled with him onto the shell-covered beach, landing on her bottom with an ungainly bump, her legs flying in the air. Matt fell on top of her, his hands either side of her head, staring down into her eyes, his mouth inches from hers, his breath coming in spurts from the exertion of catching up with her.

Rosie felt as though that moment stretched on forever as each waited for the other to react. The surrounding world receded from view and all that she wanted was for Matt to kiss her. She didn't have to wait a second longer to feel his lips on hers, soft and gentle at first, holding a question. She lifted her head from the sand and kissed him back.

Matt needed no more convincing. He snaked his palm around her neck, kissing her properly, and her heart soared with exhilaration as an avalanche of emotion tumbled through her. Matt broke away, his lips moving towards her cheek. The warmth of his breath as he whispered in her ear sent a multi-tude of exquisite sensations rippling down her spine and exploding somewhere in her lower abdomen.

'You're shivering. Come on. I've got a couple of beach towels in the SUV.'

The last thing Rosie wanted to do was break out of their personal beachside bubble, but Matt was right, she had started to shake and whilst she would have liked to say it was from desire, she was acutely aware of goose bumps tingling all over her skin. Matt pushed himself up and offered her his hand. She took it with a smile and they dashed back to the car park, laughing as she tried to put on her shoes whilst she ran – not an easy task.

Back at the car, Matt wrapped her in a huge bright purple towel and settled her in the passenger seat, turning the heater on full blast. Within minutes she felt better, but her hair had other ideas and morphed into its habitual imitation of copper-coloured candyfloss. She ran her fingers through its bulk which only made it worse so she gave up. To her surprise, she suddenly felt awkward. She knew Matt was watching her, waiting for her to say something but for some reason her mind had gone completely blank. Matt was the first person she had kissed since finding Harry rolling amongst the shrubbery at the flower shop. Was she ready to hand her heart over to someone again?

But Matt wasn't Harry. She remembered that his relation-ship history was probably even more distressing than her own. He had been ready to marry his soulmate when Victoria had ditched him in the worst possible, and most public, of ways.

She had no way of knowing what was going through his own head as he stared out of the windscreen at the view beyond.

And what a view it was! The sky had turned a glorious shade of pink, tinged with ripples of salmon where the sea met the land. The undulating sand dunes took on a bleached white colour with sprigs of coarse grasses poking out like a giant's ear hairs. Rosie glanced across at Matt but his eyes remained fixed on the horizon, his arms draped over the steering wheel, his expression tense. His lips had tightened and his Adam's apple trembled at his throat as he struggled to reign in his emotions.

'My dad loved it here. He used to bring Mum to this precise spot when they were dating. He used to say "how can anyone not fall in love when they look at that view". He passed away ten years ago and I still miss him every single day, but I know he'd hate it if I allowed my grief to prevent me from grabbing the chance to enjoy every single minute of what life has to offer. How do you know what you can achieve unless you take a leap into the unknown? We might fall flat on our faces – and heaven knows I've done that lots of times – but we might just get to soar.'

'Your father sounds like an amazingly perceptive man, Matt.'

'He was the most fantastic guy you could ever wish to meet. I reckon he managed to squeeze two lifetimes into his forty-eight years. He completed the Three Peaks challenge five times, he cycled the Coast-to-Coast three times and hiked the Pennine Way, but the thing he loved the most was rock climbing. You name it – Snowdonia, the Lake District, the Scottish Highlands, the Pyrenees, the Alps – he just had to climb the highest peak. It was more than a weekend hobby, it was a kind of obsession; as though the mountain was a vengeful monster standing in his way and he couldn't rest until he'd tamed it.'

Matt paused, preparing himself to deliver the most difficult of words.

'But there was one monster he couldn't tame – the Eiger. He knew the dangers, but insisted on tackling it anyway. There's a reason it's called The Murder Wall – everyone in his climbing party perished after a heavy rockfall wiped them from its surface. I was twenty-one when the accident happened, waiting for my degree results before taking up my place at Hendon. Mum couldn't be expected to run the outward-bound centre on her own, could she? So, along with Freddie – who'd just failed all his A levels because of his parents' divorce – I stepped into my dad's very large boots with trepidation and took on the responsibility of managing Ultimate Adventures. I hope I've done enough over the last decade to make him proud.'

Rosie gulped down on her emotions, reaching over to squeeze Matt's hand as she too was bombarded by painful memories. She was surprised that their stories had so many similarities.

'You know, I felt so guilty when he died. It wasn't my fault, of course, I know that, but with the benefit of hindsight I realized how hurt he must have been when I told him I wanted to pursue a career in the police force instead of joining him at Ultimate Adventures. After all, he'd built the business up single-handedly so that he could hand it over to his sons. And

I *do* love it! I love that every day is different, that I can spend most of my time in the great outdoors, close to nature, and that I get to work with a great bunch of people. Dad was right – I would have hated to be cooped up in an office, filling in paperwork, battling with bureaucracy and struggling with the networking that's required to climb the career ladder. I really wish I could tell him.'

'Matt, you can't blame yourself for what happened. *I* know that.'

Matt had no reason to suspect, but she knew exactly how he was feeling. She wanted to confide in him about her own teenage dreams, that unlike him she *had* wanted to follow in her father's footsteps by training as a criminal defence lawyer. She wanted to tell him about her own obsession with detective novels, too, but that meant talking about her father and she wasn't sure if she was ready to embark on that journey.

'Dad set up Ultimate Adventures so he could share his enthusiasm for outdoor pursuits with other people and he liked nothing more than convincing the most reluctant of clients that they could do anything if they were only prepared to put in a little bit of effort. But he always said that his proudest achievement was raising his family.'

Tears gathered along Rosie's lower lashes as she saw the sadness in Matt's eyes, but her breath was coming in shortened spurts as she contemplated opening up her own heart. She might have been able to paper over the cracks the loss of her father had caused, but she had not yet been able to decorate them with her choice of pastel-coloured paint. Yet Matt had talked about his father tackling monsters; maybe it was time she started to tackle some of her own and sitting there next to Matt she felt so calm, so comfortable in his presence, that she knew she could say anything and he would completely understand.

She clenched her fists and inhaled a deep, fortifying breath. When she eventually spoke, her voice sounded alien to her ears, as though someone else was speaking the words, recounting a story somehow. But then that was exactly what it was, her own *story*.

'My dad died when I was fourteen. It was a huge shock, so unexpected that it sent our world into turmoil. Mum was so devastated she couldn't function for weeks and my sister and I were cared for by our aunt. The doctors told us it was a heart attack, brought on by the stress caused by his job as a commercial litigation solicitor. He had always worked long hours, sometimes even all night; we just thought that was normal. Whenever he did have some spare time, though, he would spend it devouring detective novels, hunting out new authors to share with me so we could have a reading race to guess whodunnit. Dad's other hobby was his garden which he used to get away from the pressures of work. I inherited my love of plants and flowers from him. It's... it's where he died. I... I... found him collapsed in the greenhouse where he'd been tending his tomato plants. I'll never be able to erase that image from my memory.'

Rosie exhaled and allowed her tears to flow down her cheeks and the memories of that painful time to bombard her. She had thought her life had ended that day when she had watched the paramedics take her father away in the ambulance. She had begged to be allowed to go with him and her mother, but she and Georgina had been ushered into a neighbour's house until their aunt arrived to collect them. It had been the worst two hours of her life.

'Rosie, I'm so, so sorry.'

Matt slipped his palm into hers and squeezed. The gesture gave her the courage to continue. Now that she had started, she wanted to finish the story, to excavate every last morsel of pain from her soul and propel it out into the open where it could start to live, and hopefully grow old and less vibrant.

'Mum struggled to come to terms with her grief, but no one knew how bad things had become until the house was repossessed and we had to move to a tiny flat above a bakery in another part of Hampshire. Georgie and I had to change schools so we lost all our friends and our support network. I was fifteen, still mourning my dad and trying to bolster my mum's spirits and make sure Georgie was fed.'

Rosie wasn't surprised to find that her recollections of that agonizing time were still as sharp as if they had occurred yesterday. She remembered with absolute clarity the heavy physical ache that had lodged in her chest like a block of concrete, refusing to budge no matter how hard she tried.

'I didn't fail my exams, but I didn't get the grades I needed to continue with my dream of becoming a lawyer. I was fortunate that one of the teachers at my new school took pity on me and guided me towards my second love – baking. The owner of the bakery downstairs from our flat gave me a Saturday job and I learned everything there was to know about creating stunning cakes from her. I think my obsession with hygiene was born around this time. It was my way of putting some order into my otherwise chaotic life. If we couldn't do anything else, at least we could have a clean and tidy home, and there was plenty of food on the table, even if it was leftovers from the bakery.'

'Rosie, I can't begin to imagine how difficult this was for you.'

'I didn't think about it at the time. I just knew I had to get on with things. I went to the local catering college – which I loved – and life took on a different kind of normality. Mum started to emerge from her melancholy and joined a support group for bereaved spouses who introduced her to a swimming club which she loves. They even went on a "club trip" to Austria in July so they could swim in one of the lakes. Georgie made new friends at school and our little family chugged along like any other – trying its best to make sure everything worked out. I met Harry when I was working as a pastry chef in a hotel in Winchester. He had the contract to provide the flower arrangements but he'd always dreamed of having his own business, which he achieved a year later in Pimlico. So I grabbed onto the coattails of his dreams and joined him, learning how to be a florist as I went along. That didn't work out either, as you know.'

Rosie hadn't realized it but whilst she had been baring her soul, the sun had exhaled its last breath and dipped behind the horizon. Dusk washed the scene in a shadowy filter, but it was still beautiful. She felt exhausted, as though every scrap of energy had seeped from her veins and left her totally depleted. However, she also felt a huge sense of relief – that by recounting her history to a sympathetic listener she had halved her burden. The fact that she had left nothing out, had even admitted that her problem with cleanliness had stemmed from the loss of her father and not from her relationship breakdown, had answered her own questions.

She swivelled in her seat to face Matt, his hand still firmly clamped in hers. She smiled and a huge swathe of gratitude washed over her. Whilst she wouldn't say she was euphoric, she felt buoyant, as though an ancient curse had been lifted, and she knew that from now on the only way she'd look was forward.

'Thank you, Matt.'

'What for?'

'For this. For listening to me. For holding my hand and letting me talk. For not judging me. Well, for being Matt.'

'Rosie, it's absolutely my pleasure. But please don't forget that you've done the same for me. Relationships are a two-way street. We give and we take without the need of gratitude.'

Matt held her eyes and slowly leaned forward until his lips met hers and they kissed until there was no light left in the car – but the light of life shone brightly in Rosie's mind.

Chapter 19

St Andrew's Church was the focal point of village life in Willerby. The whole community revolved around its church hall and the door to the vicarage was always open to anyone who required the sage advice of its occupants. A row of old stone cottages, with honeysuckle and clematis weaving their way around their doors, framed the village green that was still bedecked with strings of pastel-coloured bunting flapped in the breeze. Streetlamps cast their amber light over the bucolic scene, enhancing the golden aura that seemed to encircle the buildings.

The carpark at the Drunken Duck was crammed with a jumble of assorted vehicles and the cycle rack overflowed as testament to the quality of the beer on offer. Rosie jumped from Matt's SUV and smiled when she caught sight of the silver bowl on the pub's stone doorstep offering a drink of water to any passing thirsty hound. Together they crossed the road to the quaint kissing gate which led into the churchyard.

'Are you sure about this?' Rosie asked, scrutinizing Matt's expression carefully. 'We could ask Suki and Jess to meet us at the pub?'

'How can I expect bravery from others if I'm not prepared to stand up and fight my own monsters?'

Matt smiled at her and reached out to unfasten the wooden gate. Rosie slipped her hand into his and together they navigated the winding pathway towards the vicarage. Weeds and grass sprouted like wiry whiskers from between the cracks and the overhanging beech trees provided an arboreal tunnel to the front door, its cheery facade welcoming them with a burst of fragrance from the pale pink roses draped across the lintel.

It was the perfect sanctuary for Suki and Jess, away from the turmoil of the last few days. Rosie also knew that, just like Suki and Jess, Carole and Roger Coulson were no strangers to heartache. She had heard from Mia that they had lost their youngest daughter, Harriet, to meningitis when she was only seven and they bore their grief with dignity, coupled with a staunch belief in hope and the healing power of love. Knowing their story had made Rosie realize that she wasn't the only person on whom fate had unceremoniously dumped its load of anguish and pain – that particular party was peopled by even the most undeserving of gate-crashers.

Matt knocked on the door and Rosie felt a lurch of pleasure when Carole's cheerful face appeared to welcome them in. A pleasant aroma, a fusion of warm caramel and golden syrup, of furniture polish and kindness, emanated from the house.

'Oh, hello, Matt. It's good to see you. Come in, come in. Suki and Jess are in the lounge, but you'll have to excuse me. My daughter Grace is arriving with her boyfriend tonight. They're planning to go midnight hiking and they want to stock up on carbs.' Carole rolled her eyes in mock irritation. 'You'd think they were climbing Kilimanjaro the amount of equipment they need to take with them to scramble through the heather. Roger is busy brushing up on his obligatory health and safety lecture about the dangers of camping in the wild. I don't have the heart to tell him about the quality of the accommodation the two of them stayed in whilst travelling in Cambodia and Thailand over the summer and that they're quite used to roughing it.'

'I don't envy them at all,' said Rosie. 'I'd say I'm more into rambling than scrambling! Wish them luck from me.'

'Will do. Tea? And maybe a slice of coffee and walnut cake?'

'Count me in,' beamed Matt, seemingly completely relaxed for his first visit to Carole's kitchen since he'd availed himself of her services when he'd been a jilted groom.

'Coming right up.'

Rosie pushed open the door into the lounge and Jess rushed forward to greet her with a hug while Suki looked on with a weak smile.

'Thanks for coming. I'm sorry to ask you to come to the vicarage, but now that the police are getting involved I'll admit to being a little scared.'

'No problem.'

Rosie settled herself down on Carole's flowery sofa and Matt took a leather armchair next to the fireplace, currently empty of flames. The living room had clearly not yet been released from the embrace of the Eighties' craze for all things country chic. Soft furnishings were obviously Carole's domain, and she had been given a free hand to indulge her creative urges, probably to diminish the impact of the dreary portraits of Roger's scowling clerical predecessors which lined the hallway. Every available surface boasted evidence of Carole's obsession with ceramics and a vividly swirled purple carpet and pink velvet curtains completed the look. Yet, to Rosie, the entire house felt as though it had been draped in a mantle of comfort and compassion, embroidered with a seam of faith in the power of friendship.

'Oh, hello Alfie.'

The dog bypassed Matt and made a beeline for Rosie who fondled the ears of the lively Lhasa Apso bundle of white fur.

'Tea and cake,' announced Carole, putting a tray down on the coffee table and then leaving them to their discussions.

'So, what did you want to talk to us about?' asked Matt, grabbing a plate and a slice of the still-warm coffee cake.

'Felix seems to think you're looking into how that weird stuff got into my throat spray.'

'Oh, well, we just wanted to...' began Rosie, feeling like a village busybody.

'No, sorry, don't get me wrong. I *want* you to ask questions and if you find anything out, I want you to tell me immediately. I think that whoever did put something in my spray didn't mean for me to get so ill, just wanted to either stop me from performing at the Windmill Café after the garden party, or perhaps when I *did* try to sing, my voice would be awful. What I don't know is who – and it can only be one of four people.'

'Four?' asked Jess. 'Are you counting Lucas then?'

'Sorry, Jess.'

'But it can't be Lucas. Why would he do that?'

'Why would anyone?'

'I suppose so.'

Before Rosie could ask all the questions she had stored up for just such an opportunity, the door opened again and Carole popped her head inside the lounge.

'Suki, dear, I'm so sorry to bother you, but do you think you could come into the kitchen for a few minutes and meet a couple of the ladies from the local WI committee? We're just wondering if you'd be interested in giving a talk at our next meeting about your road to stardom?'

Suki smiled and pushed herself up from the sofa. 'Sorry, guys, back in a minute. Jess, will you tell Rosie and Matt what we were thinking?'

'Sure.'

Suki left the room and Rosie turned back to Jess who looked just like an undernourished waif as she hunched against the chintzy cushions of the sofa, twisting a strand of her beaded hair. She wore distressed jeans cut off at the knee and a peasant-style blouse with brightly coloured tassels along the hem. She looked as though she hadn't slept for weeks which added to Rosie's impression of a frightened schoolgirl as she simply stared wide-eyed at Matt, waiting for him to start the conversation.

'I think Suki is right, Jess. Apart from her friends, no one else at the party had any idea that she relied on her throat spray before performing.'

'But who would want to do such an awful thing? Everyone adores Suki. She's the kindest, the most caring person...' Her voice rasped and she attempted to clear her throat. 'Do you think… do you think someone *was* actually trying to *kill* her?'

'No, of course not,' said Rosie, moving to sit in the seat vacated by Suki and taking hold of the young girl's hand.

'But why would they want to hurt her? It doesn't make any sense.'

'What about Suki's relationship with Felix?' asked Matt.

'Oh, that was fizzling out even before we decamped to Ibiza.' Jess's pale blue eyes took on a wary expression and Rosie knew immediately that she had known about William. 'But Felix wouldn't do anything to harm her!'

'Do you think he realized things were cooling off?'

'You know, don't you?' asked Jess, fiddling with the handle of her mug before releasing a long, agony-filled sigh. 'Suki was seeing William. She felt guilty about Nadia, of course, but she loved William. She went out to his parents' tennis academy at the beginning of May and that's when she realized she had feelings for him. If you ask me, William has always loved Suki, but it was the "ping" moment for her. She should have broken it off with Felix straightaway but she refused. She didn't want to hurt Nadia. She was so conflicted. Like I said, she's a good person. She's the best sister anyone could ask for and all this is so upsetting.'

Jess's voice cracked and she crumpled into Rosie's arms. It was several minutes before she raised her head and was able to continue.

'Suki has always adored music, you know, from the very first moment she bashed a pan with a wooden spoon. She believes that music is the source of true happiness, that the songs she writes can offer meaning to those who give them the opportunity to live. She wants to devote her time to sharing her gift with others in the hope that the pleasure she feels when she sings can also fill her listeners' hearts with joy – her words not mine.'

'Do you mind telling us a bit about your family's trust fund?'

'I don't know much about it. Suki handles all our finances with Uncle Ken – Dad's older brother. The money we inherited was put in trust until we reach twenty-five. Suki's just got control of her share. She used some of it to update her wardrobe, bought some decent sound equipment, and had a few voice coaching sessions. She isn't a big spender. That's my forte. I've been spoiled, I know. I'm a huge responsibility for Suki, but she never complains. She wanted me to get a job when I finished uni, learn the value of earning my own money, but I just wanted to party. As soon as we get back to London, I'm going to look for an internship at one of the big publishers.'

Rosie had been so engrossed in what Jess had been saying that she hadn't noticed Suki had returned to the lounge.

'I'm sorry, Jess, we're not leaving Norfolk until I find out what's going on.'

Chapter 20

Darkness draped the rooftops of Willerby when Matt and Rosie left the vicarage. Matt stretched his shoulders and rubbed his thumb and finger over the bridge of his nose in an effort to relieve the tension that had built up there.

'So, how was it? Your first visit to the vicarage?' said Rosie, linking her arm through Matt's.

'Not as bad as I expected.'

'It never is. Come on. I'll treat you to a lemonade at the Drunken Duck.'

The pub had emptied of the hordes who had descended for their evening meal. Only the local stalwarts remained, hunched over their pint as though they expected it to deliver the answers to all life's questions and were saddened when it didn't.

'Hi, you two,' said Mia plonking herself down next to Rosie. 'Freddie's getting the drinks in. Don't worry, mine's a Coke. I heard from the grapevine that the café will be back up and running tomorrow and I want to be at my best. I'm itching to get stuck in to baking again and I've got a few new recipes I want to try out. Oh, Rosie, it's such a relief to know that

197

our beloved little Windmill Café had nothing to do with what happened. So, are you going to leave the investigations up to the police now?'

'Probably,' said Matt.

'No way!' exclaimed Rosie, shocked at Matt's swift acquiescence. 'Whoever did this to Suki, did it to the Windmill Café too and I intend to stick it out to the end and see the poisoner gets what he or she deserves! We might as well finish what we started – despite the fact that I've actually ruled out everyone we've spoken to so far and we've only got Lucas left to talk to.'

'Yes, but like Jess said, it's unlikely to be him.'

'My money's still on Nadia – *hell hath no fury* and all that,' said Mia.

'Or the *guy* spurned,' muttered Freddie, setting down the drinks and taking a long draught of his Guinness.

'Mia, I don't think it's Nadia. She's had ample opportunity to slip something into Suki's throat spray, or anything else for that matter, when they were singing together in Ibiza. She's also known about the record deal and the affair for weeks, so why wait until now? And don't you think she would steer clear of something as obvious as putting poison in the spray because the spotlight would fall on her immediately?'

Rosie sipped the red wine Freddie had bought her as she fought her way through the forest of contradictory thoughts cluttering her mind.

'So, why don't you think it could be Felix?' Freddie asked.

'He had just proposed to Suki, so he obviously wanted a future with her, and he craves the limelight so much I don't think he would do anything to jeopardize his chance of being the other half of a celebrity couple. It's his dream come true. If Felix was going to attack anyone I think it would be William, don't you?' said Matt.

'Okay, so it looks like we've exhausted the "love" angle as a motive,' Rosie accepted reluctantly, recalling her wager with Matt early on in their investigation. 'I suppose we need to turn to the "money" angle now.'

'I agree, but I have no idea how to do that.'

'Leave it with me. When our family home was repossessed, Dad's brother, Uncle Martyn, did our conveyancing for free, and because he knew I was interested in qualifying as a solicitor, he invited me into his office to show me how the process worked. I remember he carried out a couple of searches before we bought the flat which revealed information about the vendor's financial background. I could give him a call and ask if he's got any advice.'

'That's great! I'll try to do some digging too.'

'Well, no time like the present!'

Rosie grabbed her phone and made her way outside to the dimly lit courtyard at the rear of the pub. She searched her contacts for her uncle's number and waited for him to answer. She was disappointed when her call went to voicemail, but she decided to leave him a very precise message about what she was looking for. Like herself, Martyn had always been a very practical person, able to slice through the jumble of irrelevant information and arrive at the nub of the matter with the least amount of fuss. She briefly wondered if her tendency towards orderliness could be genetic rather than psychological, but she had enough to contend with at the moment without embarking on a random course of self-diagnosis.

'So, can you email me anything that's thrown up, please?'

She terminated her call as a blast of homesickness took her by surprise. She made a pact to visit her Uncle Martyn and Aunt Beatrice in their cosy thatched cottage in Somerset just as soon as the current crisis was over. She knew both of them would be fascinated to hear what had been going on. She made her way back to the pub, the warm air and convivial atmosphere hitting her like an errant hairdryer.

'You know, the only person you've not had a conversation with is Lucas. Are you going to talk to him?' asked Mia, warming to their theme. 'Oooh, this is just like an episode of Midsomer Murders.'

'Except for one thing.'

'What's that?'

'Thankfully no one was murdered!'

'Oh, yes!' Mia giggled and Freddie rolled his eyes.

'But why would Lucas want to prevent Suki from singing?'

'No idea, but we should try and have a chat with him, if we can, just to complete the picture.'

'Okay, that's enough mystery-solving for one night. While you were over interviewing suspects at the vicarage, Freddie and I have been chatting to Grace and Josh. Did Carole tell you they're going wild camping tonight? I've been trying to persuade Freddie that we should join them. Oh, and Rosie, you should see Grace's engagement ring. It's amazing. They're getting married at St Andrew's on Christmas Eve – how romantic is that?'

Mia flashed a quick look at Freddie as she said that, but he was oblivious to the cryptic message. Rosie smiled, happy that there was perhaps another budding romance in their midst even if one of the protagonists didn't know it. Mia deserved her fairy tale ending and she truly hoped Freddie would wake up and at least ask her for a date.

'Maybe you should start dating again, Rosie?'

Despite having prepared herself over the last four months for that very question, it still hit Rosie with unexpected force. She felt warmth spread into her cheeks and she didn't dare meet Matt's eyes, although she could feel them on her. Yes, she and Matt had shared a couple of kisses on the beach, but that didn't mean they were writing the next epic love story. It was way too soon to be talking about dating and she didn't want any pressure from her friends to rush into anything that might turn out to be a mistake.

'Maybe.'

Rosie saw Freddie roll his eyes before he quickly excused himself to help Matt with the drinks. However, she had an inkling that Mia might just have sown a seed in the shadowy crevices of his mind where it would lay dormant until she could coax it into the light when the conditions became more favourable. She smiled whilst simultaneously scouring her brain for a change of subject, terrified Mia would continue with the dating conversation and unearth the details of her and Matt's afternoon on the beach. Fortunately, Matt arrived back with a tray of drinks just in time.

'Where's Freddie disappeared off to? I've just seen him head out to the car park.'

'I think he might have needed a breath of fresh air,' laughed Rosie.

'Okay,' said Matt, looking from Rosie to Mia and back again. 'What's going on?'

'I think we can safely assume that it will be a few weeks before Freddie is happy to start dating again. He's still getting over the shock of what happened with Suki, but when he does, I reckon there might be a queue!'

'And guess who's going to be first in line?'

'He's a lucky guy.' Matt smiled. 'Come on, Detective Constable Barnes. Let's finish these drinks and I'll give you a lift home. It's been one of the longest days since... erm... since I can remember.'

Rosie knew what he was going to say but was pleased to note that the moment passed swiftly with no accompanying flash of sadness. If Matt was starting to refer to what had happened between him and Victoria in general conversation then it was a good sign. She too felt that the next time she and Mia went out for a few well-deserved cocktails in Norwich, she would be able to talk to her friend about the details of how she found out about Harry's cheating, to rake over the embers of her pain until they no longer glowed with such intensity.

They exchanged farewells and Rosie and Matt left the pub, crossing the road to where Matt had left his vehicle. Rosie caught his arm and pulled him back into the shadows of the vicarage kissing gate.

'Mmm, an assignation under the kissing gate?'

Rosie wished she had thought of that but it was something else.

'Isn't that Lucas? What's he doing hanging around the vicarage this late? You don't think he's spying on Jess and Suki, do you?'

Matt followed Rosie's eyeline and as they watched on from their vantage point behind Matt's SUV, Lucas took out his phone and engaged in an animated call.

'Why would he want to spy on them? He's probably on chauffeur duty like me, but it's something we can ask him about it when we talk to him.' Matt grinned as he opened the door to allow Rosie to clamber into the passenger seat. 'You're enjoying this sleuthing game, aren't you?'

'It brings back all the best memories of the time I spent with my dad. I wish he was here so I could ask him for his ideas on what's happened at the café, and to share my theories with him. I bet he would have had *The Mystery of the Poisoned Throat Spray* solved in five seconds flat.'

Chapter 21

A n insistent buzzing noise drew Rosie from a dream-filled slumber. Until the events at the garden party on Sunday, sleep had no longer been the elusive yet necessary oblivion from her demons she had craved after leaving Pimlico. She could usually enjoy a restful night and wake feeling refreshed and excited about the day ahead. She was grateful for her cosy home above the little Windmill Café – her sojourn in its comfortable confines had set her on the path to recovery from the heartbreak Harry had caused.

She prised open her eyelids and raised her head, surprised to find her pillow was unusually hard and warm. When she lifted her palm to pat it into shape, the recollection hit her square in the face – she had persuaded Matt to come up to her flat for a brandy and she must have fallen asleep on his chest. Cautiously she glanced downwards, relief surging through her body when she saw that she was still wearing her very crumpled T-shirt from the day before. She needed time to explore her feelings about her blossoming friendship with Matt before taking their relationship any further. However, from the way her heart fluttered with interest when she raised her eyes to his face, surfer-dude handsome in repose, she knew her deliberations wouldn't take very long at all.

The buzzing sound stopped and she belatedly realized it had been her phone ringing. She checked the screen to see who was calling her so early in the morning, but the caller ID had been blocked. Oh, well, if it was important they would ring back.

She decided to leave Matt to sleep and jumped into the shower. Under the cascade of hot water, she took the opportunity to continue to chase every implausible theory of what might have happened through the labyrinths of her mind. It was Thursday. Suki and her friends were due to check out that morning, but Suki was still insisting on staying in Norfolk until the police had caught the person responsible. Who knew how long that would be? Why couldn't they have solved the mystery so Suki and her party could be on their way, vacating their lodges for the next set of guests arriving the following day.

And there was another thing piling on the pressure – how was Graham going to react when he flew in, at last, from Barbados later that day? Would the Windmill Café really be able to overcome the scandal without a definitive explanation of what had happened? And if not, would Graham feel he had no alternative but to terminate her employment so the café could make a fresh start without her at the helm? This time tomorrow, would she not only be looking for a new job, but a new place to live?

Also, she was deeply grateful to Matt for giving up so much of his time to delve into the mystery but if he didn't get back to running his own business, that might suffer too and she couldn't allow that. She had only met him a few months ago but she felt as though she had known him forever. In fact, she would even go as far as to say that whenever she was in Matt's company she felt more alive than she had ever felt with Harry, that the world around her existed in glorious technicolour rather than tinted sepia.

She dressed quickly, dried her hair, and forced a smile onto her lips as she filled the kettle for her first coffee of the day. As she waited for the water to boil, she stared out of the window, watching the dawn roll over the horizon spreading cerulean and ivory light over the wide expanse of sea. The sunrise seemed to be even more beautiful that day – probably because she knew it might be her last chance to enjoy it – and she wondered why she hadn't made more of an effort to witness the spectacle every morning.

'Mmm, that coffee smells good.'

Rosie handed Matt a mug of the fragrant brew and leaned back against the countertop, hugging her own between her palms, her heart racing as she took a moment to appreciate the man in front of her, his untidy hair and unshaved jawline doing nothing to detract from his gorgeousness. She felt heat surge into her cheeks when he saw the effect his proximity was having on her and to cover her embarrassment she glanced again at her phone to see there was a text from the unknown caller.

Her curiosity piqued, she scanned the missive quickly.

'It's a text from my Uncle Martyn. He says he's sent me an email.'

This time her pounding heart had nothing to do with Matt breathing over her shoulder as she opened the email her uncle had sent her a few moments ago from his solicitors' practice in Bath. She scanned the contents and then clicked to open the first of two attachments labelled financial search. One of the names on the document leapt out at her.

'It looks like you were right all along, Matt! Suki *was* targeted for her money – which means the perpetrator didn't just want to prevent Suki from singing, they wanted to... wanted to kill her! Oh my God!'

A spasm of shock blasted through Rosie's chest, so strong it squashed the air from her lungs. She gasped for breath and had to grip the back of a chair until she was able to crumple into its seat at her kitchen table. Her fingers trembled on the handle of her mug and a wave of nausea threatened to overwhelm her. A tumble of 'what ifs' crashed through her mind as she fought to bring the thump of her heartbeat under control.

'Hang on, Rosie. Just because a person is unfortunate enough to have been made bankrupt doesn't mean they would plot to kill someone for their money.'

'True, but now take a look at this.' She showed Matt the second attachment. 'Look at the second line on the certificate – see the qualification?'

Had Rosie not been so overwhelmed by what she saw she would have smiled at the thoroughness of her uncle's attempt to obtain every piece of information available on her chosen subject – especially as it looked like he'd been working on his factual excavations into the early hours. No wonder he had been so popular with the criminal fraternity of Somerset for the last thirty-five years.

'I see it... oh, do you think... that's why they chose that particular poison?'

'Of course, and they would have known that the effects would be instantaneous. I can't believe it, I really can't.'

'Rosie, what your uncle had discovered is very convincing, but you do know it's pure speculation, don't you? It's not hard evidence that links anyone to a crime.'

Rosie's bubble of excitement burst and her elation at what she had uncovered vanished. Matt had the decency to look contrite; after all, the new information they had gleaned meant they could continue to pursue their suspicions in the knowledge they were on the right track.

'Look, I've got a friend who runs a rock climbing school in Ibiza. Why don't I ask him to make a few subtle enquiries? See if he stumbles on anything interesting? In the meantime, I think we should go straight to the police with what we know and they can decide what to do about it.'

'But what about the café? We're supposed to be reopening at eleven o'clock.'

'Okay, I'll go to the police and you stay at the café and carry on as normal. Mia will be here soon, but maybe it'll be best if you don't say anything to her. Whatever happens, don't let anyone in Suki's party leave. I know Suki and Jess intend to stay on, but that doesn't mean the rest of them will. Do whatever's necessary – offer them brunch on the house, or suggest another of those impromptu baking sessions, just make sure they don't go until I get back. Okay?'

'Yes, no problem.'

Rosie suddenly had a vision of her grappling with the culprit as they tried to escape from her clutches and make their getaway, forcing her to chase after them, whisk in one hand, spatula in the other, until she wrestled them to the ground in the car park, tying their hands with a length of bunting and accepting the appreciative applause of Mia and Freddie. But then reality invaded her crime-thriller drama and her stomach began to churn with fear.

'You will come straight back, won't you?'

But Matt was already half way to the car park, his ear fixed firmly to his phone as he called his friend in Ibiza. Rosie watched him go, enjoying the whiff of his aftershave that still lingered in the air and had accompanied her to sleep the previous night.

Would the information her uncle had uncovered be enough for the police to hotfoot it down to the Windmill Café to arrest the person who had poisoned Suki? She hoped so because if everything could be neatly tied up before Graham arrived from the airport, she might just be able to keep her job – and her home.

And now that Matt Wilson was in her life, there was nothing she wanted more.

Chapter 22

It was 9.30, and the birds were well into the second rendition of their daily overture, celebrating the warmth of the late summer morning. The breeze had chased the earlier clouds away and the clear blue sky promised that the next few hours would be filled with sunshine. To keep herself from descending into a torrent of panic, Rosie had decided to do what she did best and bake. By the time Mia arrived for her shift, she had already made a batch of coffee and walnut cupcakes, two dozen chocolate and crushed pecan cookies and a huge jug of homemade lemonade.

'Is there something wrong, Rosie?'

'What makes you say that?'

'You've just sprinkled pepper instead of nutmeg on top of those cupcakes.'

'Oh, sorry.'

'And I've just seen Matt talking to Suki in the car park and she was crying.'

Rosie swallowed down her anxiety and fixed a cheerful smile on her face, but she knew she wasn't fooling Mia. She had never been top of the class when it came to acting skills and anyway, Mia was nothing if not astute when reading people's emotions. Today her friend had turned up for work in a pair of white dungarees, cut off at the knee, and a peppermint T-shirt to match the windmill café's signature colours. Her apron, however, spoilt the whole outfit because it was festooned with kittens in pink bows cavorting amongst yellow sunflowers.

'I wasn't going to say anything until we...'

'Hi Rosie, hi Mia,' mumbled Jess, appearing on the threshold, her usual joie de vivre missing-in-action. 'Matt's told us to come down to the café at 10.00.'

'Ordered us, you mean! I don't know who he thinks he is, but...'

'Leave it, Felix,' snapped Suki.

Rosie realized that Matt must have shared what he had found out with Suki, and yet she was still shocked at her appearance. Gone was the polished, glossy exterior she had presented when she arrived, to be replaced by swollen eyes and skin so pale that it held a bluish tinge. She looked like a hunted animal, exhausted from the chase, her demeanour shrunken as she and Jess huddled together on one of the café's white leather sofas. In a reversal of roles, Suki had her arm linked through Jess's as though, this time, she needed every ounce of strength her sister could offer her.

A stab of intense sympathy shot through Rosie as her memory zoomed back to the day she had been told her beloved father had died whilst tending his plants. For days, no, weeks afterwards every single action she was required to perform was a huge chore, so that just walking to school was like wading through treacle, every thought clouded in a mist of confusion. She knew this was how Suki was feeling and that she was only holding herself together by the force of her will.

'How long is this going to take?' asked Lucas, dropping down into one of the hard-backed chairs, his ankle resting on his knee, hands behind his head as though he didn't have a care in the world, sending a confident wink across to Jess who returned it with a nervous smile. 'Mmm, these cookies are delicious. Want one, Nad?'

Nadia ignored him and choose a seat on the sofa opposite Suki and Jess, watching as William sat down next to her, the space between them a chasm of bitterness and resentment. Devoid of the heavy makeup she preferred, Nadia's face was pinched and gaunt, exhibiting none of the confidence of previous days, and for the first time she had concealed her cleavage beneath one of William's cashmere sweaters. William leaned forward in his seat, his forearms resting on his thighs, his gaze fixed on Suki. Only Felix remained standing, leaning against the wall next to the French doors, his hands thrust into the pockets of his jeans, a guarded look in his eyes as he studiously avoided making eye contact with anyone.

Rosie could feel the electricity crackle through the room and the hairs at the back of her neck began to prickle. Mia's eyes had widened as she sought to understand what was going on, and when she realized, she led Rosie to the remaining sofa.

Where was Matt? Why wasn't he here?

Rosie took a sip of her lemonade, just so she had something to do with her hands. A flicker of movement outside the window caught her eye and she squinted into the bleaching sunlight to see what it was. She couldn't see anything but heard a faint crunch of tyres on the gravel car park and realized it must have been the glint of reflected sunlight from a car windscreen. Someone had arrived in the Windmill Café's car park. It was too early to be Graham and she hoped it wasn't a customer who had missed, or ignored, the signs announcing that they would be closed until the next day. However, no one appeared and it slipped from her mind when Matt appeared at the doorway with Freddie.

'Thank you all for staying,' said Matt, glancing around the Windmill Café. 'I asked you all to come over to the café because I thought you would want to know who spiked Suki's throat spray and why. I've already spoken to Suki and she's happy for me to tell you what I've uncovered, but I couldn't have done any of it without the assistance of Rosie. Before I go any further though, because of what our investigation has revealed, there's someone else that needs to be here while I speak to you.'

Matt stepped out of the café onto the terrace and signalled to the person who was clearly waiting to be invited in. Rosie had no idea who she expected to appear but was relieved when a uniformed police officer took up position at the French doors and his superior moved into view on the terrace.

'Suki? Why are the police here?' whimpered Jess, tears trickling down her cheeks.

'It's okay, darling. There's nothing to worry about. It's just... well...'

'I'm Detective Sergeant Kirkham from Norfolk Constabulary.'

Please, if you could sit down, Mr Morgan, and listen to what Mr Wilson has to say,' ordered the police detective, pointing at William who had shot up from his seat, his tone inviting no argument. The man's bulk blocked the sunlight from streaming in through the French windows and cast a wide shadow over the room. 'Go ahead, Mr Wilson, if you please.'

Rosie saw Matt flash her a quick look. She gave him a smile of encouragement, her heart softening. She knew how much this opportunity to explain their enquiries meant to him, knew that had circumstances been different, then perhaps *he* could have been the detective sergeant waiting to arrest the perpetrator. She watched him inhale a deep breath to steady his nerves and she felt a surge of relief that soon all the trauma would be over.

'After the Windmill Café's summer garden party, Suki suffered from what we all assumed to be a severe bout of food poisoning – but all was not as it seemed. Earlier on in the afternoon, Suki had offered to perform a couple of songs for everyone on the terrace before going out for dinner. To make sure she wasn't disturbed in her lodge whilst she got ready, she grabbed Freddie and made a show of taking him back with her along with a bottle of champagne. A little afternoon delight, I think, was how Jess described it, or perhaps it was a ploy to make Felix jealous. But that wasn't the case because after only five minutes, Freddie was swiftly dispatched as Suki was expecting someone else.'

Rosie watched Freddie redden from his throat to the roots of his spiky ginger hair – she knew it would be a while, no matter how persuasive Mia was, before he got back on the dating horse. She switched her scrutiny to William who had lowered his head into his hands, bracing himself for the imminent exposure of his affair with Suki.

'The person Suki was expecting was William, who knew exactly why Suki had made such a fuss of the way she left the garden party. It was a signal for him to wait five minutes before making his own excuses and slipping away to her lodge. I think everyone knows now that Suki and William are having an affair – have been for months – and were planning on confessing their infidelity at the end of their holiday in Norfolk to allow their respective partners the opportunity to go home to their families; Felix to Colchester, Nadia to Cambridge. They shared the bottle of champagne and then William left to allow Suki to get ready for her performance.'

Nadia stood up from her place on the settee, turned toward William and swung her palm across his cheek. Rosie saw Sergeant Kirkham take a step forward so she sprang from the sofa, slid her arm around the sobbing girl's shoulders and guided her into the seat next to Mia who grabbed her hand and squeezed.

'So, did William substitute the throat spray and wait for the inevitable?' asked Matt, clearly settling into his role of narrator.

Willian stared at Matt for a few seconds, then turned to look directly at Suki, his expression serious. 'I love Suki. She's my soulmate, and I hope I'm hers. We wanted to spend those few precious moments before Felix arrived finalizing what we were going to say to him and Nadia to let them down as gently and calmly as possible. We also talked about our future together in Majorca. We even spent a couple of minutes looking at villas on the internet near to my parents' tennis academy! For God's sake, how can you even think I had anything to do with what happened to Suki? I absolutely adore her!'

The room held its breath, everyone concentrating on Matt as they awaited his pronouncement on William's fate.

'I know, and I'm sorry your plans were spoiled.'

An audible sigh of relief rippled through the café. Rosie thought it could be the rising temperature, but she had the disconcerting sensation that she had been transported to the drawing room of a 1920s murder mystery where the astute private detective held his audience in thrall as he revealed each possible theory and then discarded them one by one. She was just thinking how relieved she was that the character she had been allocated was café manager and cookie baker when she noticed Matt was looking at her, indicating Nadia with a nod of his head. She gulped, ready to refuse, but an image of her father floated across her mind and she took up the revelation baton.

'So, Nadia watches William leave the party, ostensibly to go to the bathroom; but let's assume for a moment she knows exactly where he's heading. She's known about the affair for a while and hoped that it would fizzle out when Suki's career took off. Surely a successful singer would ditch her inexperienced manager as soon as the accolades and the serious money started to roll in? Was that what you were hoping for, Nadia?'

Nadia nodded, unable to raise her eyes to meet her friend's or her boyfriend's gaze. Compassion for all three swirled around Rosie's veins and she sent a signal to Matt for him to continue with the denouement whilst she concentrated on calming her emotions.

'In fact, unbeknown to Nadia, William had been in love with Suki since university. Were your suspicions of their affair, and your jealousy of Suki's jettisoning career, enough for you to consider spiking Suki's throat spray so she would be prevented from singing, not just at the garden party, but at subsequent events? I'm sure something like that may have crossed your mind. Would William come back to you if Suki lost her record deal? Would you be able to kickstart your career with Suki out of the picture?'

All eyes, even the police sergeant's, swung in unison to where Nadia slouched, her knees drawn to her chest, tears rolling down her cheeks as she waited for Matt to answer his own questions.

'No. I don't think so.'

Once again, a collective whoosh of breath was exhaled into the room. Without waiting for another word, everyone's gaze swooped across to Felix, but clearly Matt wanted to surprise them and switched tact.

'When Dr Bairstow informed us of the presence of the toxic substance in Suki's throat spray, everyone was stumped. How could it have got there? Was it an accident or had one of the ingredients been tampered with? I have to admit it was an ingenious method of delivering an irritant to a professional singer. When we got the news that the substance was unusual – an extraction from a plant known as Devil's Helmet or monkshood – we realized that only a horticulturalist or avid gardener would have known how to source it.'

Matt left that avenue of exploration dangling for the moment. A mumble of conversation began to ripple through the gathering as everyone flicked their eyes around the room, considering and discarding each one of their friends as potential experts in the plant kingdom until their eyes came to rest on Rosie. She had never been so grateful when Matt continued speaking.

'Felix was nowhere to be seen at the garden party, despite the promises he made to Suki, because he was drinking with his friends in Colchester. He didn't arrive until minutes before we discovered Suki writhing in agony in her lodge. But was that true? What was to stop him arriving earlier and instead of joining the party, going straight to the lodge, finding Suki with William and deciding to teach her a lesson by placing an irritant in her throat spray?'

'Now look here. I don't have to stay and listen to this slanderous drivel...'

'I would rather you did, sir,' interjected Sergeant Kirkham.

Felix took one look at the bulky physique of the police officer guarding the exit and relented.

'You can sit down, Felix. I know you didn't do it,' added Matt.

'But there's no one left,' muttered Jess, her mouth covered by a scrunched-up tissue as she gulped down on the tears that she was unable to stem. 'You're not seriously suggesting that me, or Lucas, would do something to hurt Suki? She's my sister! She's the only family I have left. Without Suki, I have no one!'

Rosie saw Matt shoot a glance at Sergeant Kirkham who

removed his handcuffs from his belt and her stomach gave an uncomfortable lurch. The uniformed officer positioned himself at the French doors, his arms folded, legs apart.

Jess's eyes widened in shock, her already pale features blanched to the colour and consistency of overworked putty.

'You think it's me? You think I poisoned Suki?' she cried. 'Oh my God, why?'

'Money?' suggested Felix.

'You have no idea what you're talking about! I don't care about the stupid trust fund!' she screamed. 'I never have. Suki always gives me everything I need. I don't even know how much there is.'

'There's twenty million pounds,' said Suki, speaking for the first time, and the whole room erupted.

Chapter 23

'Please, ladies and gentlemen!' growled Detective Sergeant Kirkham. 'Quiet!'

Silence was restored immediately as everyone waited for Matt's next pronouncement. 'It's okay, Jess, I know you didn't spike Suki's spray. Lucas did.'

This time the noise level reached a crescendo of outrage. Detective Sergeant Kirkham, along with his uniformed colleague, and Freddie and Matt, moved in unison as Lucas launched out of his seat and made for the door. The sergeant wrestled him to the floor, but Lucas continued to scream and kick like a trout denied water until he was handcuffed. Freddie withdrew his Swiss army knife, severed a length of cord from one of the café's blinds, and handed it to the police constable who proceeded to tied Lucas's legs together before dragging him upright to face the Detective Sergeant.

'Lucas Julian Evans, I am arresting you for the attempted murder of Suzanne Veronica Richards. You do not have to say anything but it may harm your defence if you do not mention when questioned something which you later rely on in court. Anything you do say may be given in evidence.'

'Lucas, tell them it's not true! Tell them!' Jess wailed, rocking to and fro in Suki's arms.

'I'm sorry, Miss Richards, but we believe Mr Evans has been planning every detail of this incident for months,' said Detective Sergeant Kirkham, taking over the explanation from Matt, who, Rosie had to admit, looked exhausted. 'I've spoken to my colleagues in Ibiza and they've found suspicious compounds at the restaurant where Mr Evans works. Mr Wilson here said he thought that only a horticulturalist or avid gardener would have the requisite knowledge, but Mr Evans is a chef with a keen interest in botany. It would have been the easiest thing in the world to research a fast-acting poison, source it, and introduce it into one of your throat spray bottles.'

'But you said murder,' whimpered Jess.

'That's exactly what Mr Evans intended to do, madam,' confirmed Sergeant Kirkham. 'I understand that everyone knew Miss Richards took her spray with her wherever she went, even when she wasn't performing – as a kind of talisman. This visit to Norfolk was an ideal opportunity to put his plan into action because it had to be done before she took up her recording obligations otherwise the easy access to her personal belongings would be considerably curtailed.'

'Oh, my God!' cried Jess. 'You were going to *murder* my sister? You...'

Suki and Nadia reached out at the same time to drag Jess back down onto the sofa between them, whispering soothing words and telling her to let the police officer finish his expla-nation and then they would never have to see Lucas again. However, it was Matt who resumed the story.

'At the garden party, if you recall, Lucas made sure he was always in plain sight of everyone from the moment Suki left with Freddie. He must have thought he'd won the lottery when she decided to take a complete stranger back to her lodge – Freddie was bound to be the first person suspicion would fall on and so it proved to be the case. However, I suspect his original intention had been to leak Suki's affair with William to throw suspicion onto Felix.'

'But why? Why would you do such a thing, Lucas?' asked William, his upper lip curled in revulsion as he held Lucas's eyes before taking a seat next to Suki and drawing her into his arms. He deposited a kiss on the top of her head and turned towards Matt. 'You've covered the how and the who, but what about the why?'

'Well, it's that old cliché of money. Ever since Felix accused Rosie of poisoning the whole village with her baking, we've been trying to unravel what happened. When we found out someone had targeted Suki, we thought if we found out why, then we would find out who. You probably don't know this, but Lucas was made bankrupt last year owing more than fifty thousand pounds.'

'Lucas? Is that true?'

'I'm not saying anything.'

'He'd been bailed out several times by his mother, but he had bled her dry. Records show that she was forced to sell her home last year and has left the UK to live with her sister in Sydney. That's why Lucas took a job as a chef in a small tourist restaurant in San Antonio – so he could escape his debts and receive his wages in cash. But it seems he fell in with a bunch of gamblers at the restaurant, didn't you? How much do you owe them?'

Lucas made no attempt to answer; his eyes were trained on Jess.

'Jess, please...'

'Shut up, Lucas,' seethed William, fighting to contain his temper.

'You wanted our parents' money, did you?' shouted Jess, struggling to free herself from Suki and William's restraint. She stood in front of him, disgust written boldly across her face. 'You thought that if Suki was dead I'd be able to just hand over the cash to you? Were you intending to hang around until I turned twenty-five? That's more than four years away!'

'Jess, I had to. Those guys were threatening to shatter my kneecaps unless I came up with the funds to...'

'Will you take him away, Sergeant? I can't bear to look at him any longer,' said Suki, enveloping her sister in her arms whilst the police led Lucas from the café.

Rosie glanced at Mia who gave her a quick smile before jumping up from the sofa and rushing over to hug Freddie. She watched William, and then Felix, offer their palms to Matt, thanking him for his assistance, before leaving the café to discuss what had happened and where they went from there. She was relieved there seemed to be no animosity between the two men and she hoped that, after everything that had happened to Suki that week, she would find happiness with William.

Finally, she met Matt's gaze and a pirouette of delight wound through her body when she saw the elation and pride written across his handsome face, and maybe there was something else there in the twinkle of his eyes. Excitement joined the dance as she anticipated spending the next few hours, days or even weeks, dissecting every twist and turn of their investigation with him in the Drunken Duck. Could this be the start of a new chapter in her life, one that included not only friendship but romance? She hoped so.

'I don't know how to thank you, Rosie,' said Suki, pausing on the terrace as Jess and Nadia followed the men outside to their cars for their trip back to the airport and their flight home to their villa in Ibiza. 'Coming here to the Windmill Café just, very possibly, has saved my life.'

'Oh, well, I...'

'I want you to know that I'll be spreading the word about the gorgeous lodges you have here, and if I'm ever in the neighbourhood again, I'll be popping over for a batch of those Stilton and grape scones, and maybe another tutorial on how to make those fabulous chocolate chip cookies.'

Suki hugged Rosie, then Mia, and walked away, her shoulders straight, her head held high, every inch the superstar Rosie had no doubt she would become.

Epilogue

'So, Rosie, what did Graham say when he heard about all the excitement?' asked Freddie as he sipped his pint of Guinness in the Drunken Duck later that night. 'I assume your job is safe? After all, you and Matt have not only restored the Windmill Café's reputation – and therefore saved Graham's business from almost certain collapse – but also quite probably helped to save a rock star's life!'

'Don't worry, Freddie, Rosie's not going anywhere,' smiled Mia. 'The Windmill Café wouldn't be the same without her and Graham knows that. What about you, Matt? Have you considered ditching the outward-bound business for life as a private detective?'

'Well, if Rosie's going to be staying around here any longer, I might just have to consider that!' smirked Matt, his eyes alive with mischief. 'Do you make a habit of attracting chaos wherever you go?'

'Hey, that's not fair! How was anything that happened my fault?'

'How can you say that, Matt? Chaos is the last word I would use when describing Rosie,' laughed Freddie. 'She's a demon organizer. In fact, I've asked her to come over to Ultimate Adventures' office to see if she can help us implement some sort of filing system before our bookkeeper combusts with exasperation.'

'And did you agree?' asked Matt, his lips twitching with amusement.

'Well...'

'I'll let you do it on one condition.'

'Hey, Rosie is doing you a favour!' said Mia indignantly.

'Is it a deal?'

'Okay,' laughed Rosie.

'You come with me and Freddie on Ultimate Adventures' next wild camping expedition at the end of October.'

'Oh, I...' That had been the last thing she had expected Matt to suggest but from the way he was looking at her she knew she couldn't refuse. The more time she got to spend with Matt Wilson the better, and if that meant she had to develop an interest in outdoor sports then so be it. She would just have to stock up on antibacterial hand wash. 'Okay.'

'Rosie, do you know what you're letting yourself in for?' asked Mia, her jaw dropping in incredulity.

'Not really, but shouldn't we be prepared to try everything before we discard it?'

'Who are you and what have you done to my friend Rosie Barnes?' laughed Mia before her face grew serious. 'You do know what wild camping is, don't you? There's no tent, you collect your water from a stream, and have to carry everything you need for a night under the stars on your back!'

'Ergh!'

'No changing your mind now!' chuckled Freddie, tossing back the remainder of his pint. 'Anyway, you'll have lots of fun. After all, I know someone who'll be prepared to share his bodily warmth with you so you don't freeze to death.'

Rosie was gratified to see the colour seep into Matt's cheeks as Freddie stalked to the bar to replenish their drinks. She met his gaze and her heart ballooned at her good fortune to be able to call Matt her friend, and the possibility that he could be more than that loitered tantalizingly in the future.

'Okay, I want to propose a toast,' declared Freddie when he returned, handing round their glasses. 'To Matt and Rosie – Willerby's new crime-busting duo!'

'To Matt and Rosie!'

Rosie giggled. 'Cheers!'

Acknowledgements

A completed novel is always the result of a team effort, so I would like to say a huge, heartfelt thank you to the wonderful team at HarperImpulse, in particular my editor, Charlotte Ledger, for helping me make The Windmill Café series the best it can be.

HELP US SHARE THE LOVE!

If you love this wonderful book as much as we do then please share your reviews online.

Leaving reviews makes a huge difference and helps our books reach even more readers.

So get reviewing and sharing, we want to hear what you think!

Love, HarperImpulse x

Please leave your reviews online!

amazon.co.uk   kobo   goodreads   L♥vereading   iBooks

And on social!

f/HarperImpulse   **y**@harperimpulse
◎@HarperImpulse

LOVE BOOKS?

So do we! And we love nothing more than chatting about our books with you lovely readers.

If you'd like to find out about our latest titles, as well as exclusive competitions, author interviews, offers and lots more, join us on our Facebook page! Why not leave a note on our wall to tell us what you thought of this book or what you'd like to see us publish more of?

f/HarperImpulse

You can also tweet us 🐦@harperimpulse and see exclusively behind the scenes on our Instagram page www.instagram.com/harperimpulse

To be the first to know about upcoming books and events, sign up to our newsletter at: www.harperimpulseromance.com